The Duke Meets His Match

Infamous Somertons

The Duke Meets His Match

Infamous Somertons

TINA GABRIELLE

Entangled Publishing, LLC
2614 South Timberline Road
Suite 109
Fort Collins, CO 80525
Visit our website at www.entangledpublishing.com.

Scandalous is an imprint of Entangled Publishing, LLC.

Edited by Alycia Tornetta
Cover design by Liz Pelletier
Cover art from Period Images and iStock

Manufactured in the United States of America

First Edition July 2017

SCANDALOUS

For Laura and Gabrielle.
I love you from the moon, to the stars, to Heaven, and back.

Chapter One

On an ordinary day, Michael Keswick, the Duke of Cameron, would enjoy strolling Bullock's Museum at his leisure to study the rare Egyptian artifacts on display. He preferred being alone and disliked the foolish topics of conversation that often arose among his peers. He'd made an exception today at the request of a friend. But Henry, it seemed, had little interest in the museum, and had asked Michael to accompany him for an entirely different reason.

"What do you think of her, Your Grace?"

Michael frowned at the young man by his side. Henry may have recently inherited an earldom, but he was more than ten years his junior and lacked judgment when it came to the fair sex. He was also Michael's responsibility.

"Which one is she?" Michael said, his eyes scanning the crowded entrance.

The popular museum in Piccadilly, also known as Egyptian Hall, was renowned for its stunning architecture inspired by an Egyptian temple and vast array of curiosities from the South Seas. But Henry's gaze was not on the impressive grand hall with its pillars engraved with hieroglyphics and Egyptian symbols. Rather he was focused on two women who were admiring a reproduction of a sphinx.

"Miss Chloe Somerton is the fair-haired lady," Henry pointed out.

The women had their backs to them. Only one possessed golden hair, the object of young Henry's obsession.

"Well, then. We don't want to keep the ladies waiting, do we?" Michael started forward.

Henry placed a hand on his sleeve. "Wait. They are not expecting us."

Michael halted and narrowed his gaze at the young man. "What do you mean?"

Henry had the good sense to look uneasy. "I overheard Miss Chloe mention at Lady Holloway's ball that she would be attending the museum today with her sister, Lady Huntingdon."

Michael arched an eyebrow. "That's a bit conniving, even for you, Henry."

"I want you to meet her. Your approval is important to me, Your Grace." Henry looked at him with a mixture of admiration and hope that never failed to prick Michael's conscience.

"You shouldn't rush it, Henry. You're too young to be shackled with a wife." Michael's voice sounded harsh to his own ears.

Henry's gaze returned to the blond woman, and a lovesick look flickered in his brown eyes. "What does it matter when the lady is so fair?"

Don't let your balls rule your brains! Michael wanted to shout at Henry and shake some sense into him, right here in the middle of the museum's vestibule. How the hell was he supposed to look after the young man anyway?

The women had left the sphinx and moved on to a curiosity cabinet. From this distance, they appeared to be studying an array of Egyptian jewelry. The blonde wasn't as tall as he preferred his women, but even in the demure pink gown she wore, any man could see she was generously curved. Her golden hair was piled in an elegant style atop her head. He squinted but couldn't make out the color of her eyes. Something was vaguely familiar about her. Perhaps it was the way she walked. Head held high, almost regally, her steps fluid and graceful.

"I'll go along with your ruse," Michael said. "I know Lord Huntingdon from White's. It's an excuse to speak with his wife. Stay here until I motion for you."

Michael wove through the crowd and headed for the two women. He passed statues of Egyptian gods and goddesses, similar to the statues of Isis and Osiris that flanked the exterior of the museum. A glass dome in the ceiling cast sunlight on a temple on the Nile. But just as he neared, Lady Huntingdon wandered off to study a gold-tinted statue of a pharaoh. Chloe Somerton remained by the curiosity cabinet.

His step slowed. Should he first approach the blonde or her chaperone? He knew which was proper, but this was a strategic decision—similar to a battle plan—and he always went with his gut.

He'd been right about the cabinet's contents. Gold necklaces and earrings nestled on black velvet were displayed behind the glass. The young woman was gazing at the jewelry and didn't turn when he approached. Once again, the nagging feeling that he'd seen her before rose within him.

Michael glanced at the jewelry, then back at the lady. He cleared his throat. "Stunning."

She nodded, her attention still focused on the artifacts.

"Which is your favorite?" he asked.

She sighed. "The necklace with the turquoise scarab beetle amulet."

"Not the gold wide-collar necklace?"

"No. The workmanship of the talisman beetle is exquisite." She turned to him and smiled. "Don't you agree?"

Michael stiffened, his gaze riveted on her face.

Holy hell.

He *had* seen her before.

A few loose tendrils of golden hair had escaped her pins and brushed the slender column of her throat. Her facial bones were delicately carved, and her lips temptingly plump. But it was the sapphire eyes—exotically slanted like the pharaohs surrounding them—that made his breath hitch.

Chloe Somerton was the picture of beauty, grace, and innocence.

She was also a fraud.

He must have taken too long to answer her question. She met his gaze, and for a brief second her smile faltered, but it was back in place so quickly he imagined it a quirk of the sunlight reflecting off the glass cabinets.

"Your Grace!"

A dark-haired lady wearing a blue gown rushed forward with Henry in tow. "I'm Lady Huntingdon, Your Grace. I believe you are acquainted with my husband."

Michael bowed. "Of course. Huntingdon is an old friend." He glanced at Henry. "I'd make the introductions, but I see you've already met Lord Sefton."

"Yes. Lord Sefton and I were discussing the uniqueness of the pharaohs." She motioned to her sister. "May I introduce my sister, Miss Chloe Somerton."

The object of young Henry's interest curtsied. Chloe's bodice was trimmed with lace; just enough to display the creamy swell of her breasts. She wore no necklace, and the ivory skin at her throat was temptingly smooth. Her lips curled in a smile, revealing a dimple in her cheek, before she turned her blue gaze to meet Henry's.

Michael's protégé looked as if he would bow down to kiss her slippers.

"Lord Sefton and I previously met at Lady Holloway's ball," Chloe said. "How nice to see you again."

Something in her tone aroused Michael's suspicions. Had she known they would come? Had she devised for Henry to overhear her when she said she would be at the museum today?

The last time Michael had seen Chloe she wasn't wearing a fine gown or touring a museum. She also wasn't flirting with a young eligible gentleman who'd recently inherited an earldom.

What was her game?

"Do you have an interest in ancient Egyptian artifacts, my lord?" Chloe asked.

Henry emphatically bobbed his head. "Oh, yes. Both of us do."

"Splendid!" Lady Huntingdon clasped her hands to her chest. "I've arranged for a private tour from Mr. Bullock, the founder of the museum himself. He's a fascinating man who began as a jeweler and goldsmith before forming his collection during seventeen years of research. No one knows the museum better. Please join us."

Henry's eyes lit up as if she'd offered him all the gold in Egypt. "We'd be delighted." He glanced at Michael with a hopeful and excited expression.

Michael forced a smile. "Thank you for the gracious offer." It wasn't what he'd expected for the day, but at least he'd have a reason to observe the little charlatan and figure out her game. If she'd set her sights on Henry, then it was Michael's responsibility to look after the lad and his newly inherited fortune and title.

"We've been meaning to visit the museum since our return from Hampshire two weeks ago," Lady Huntingdon said. "But Chloe has been quite busy. She volunteers at the orphanage every Tuesday and Thursday."

"What admirable, charitable work," Henry said.

Chloe smiled sweetly. "I enjoy the children."

Michael doubted she'd know what an orphan looked like if she stumbled over one in the street. How could someone so fraudulent appear so angelic?

Mr. Bullock, the museum's founder and their guide for the afternoon, approached. A short, middle-aged man, he had a dark complexion more like a Spaniard than an Englishman. "Good day. Are you ready for your tour?"

The foursome were ushered out of the great hall, past pyramids and papyrus columns, and down a long corridor. Henry was quick to offer Chloe his arm, and his chest appeared to puff in his waistcoat when she placed the tips of her gloved fingers on his sleeve.

Michael's frown deepened. It was worse than he'd thought. The boy was already ensnared by her feminine wiles.

Mr. Bullock stopped outside an open doorway and waited for the group to enter. "This is our African room," he said, motioning to a dioramic taxidermy display of an elephant, zebra, lion, and other animals behind a roped-off section. Tall trees were also part of the display. The room was of an impressive size, and a long bench with a red cushion sat in front of the scene so one could sit and admire the animals.

"Oh my! I've never seen anything quite like this," Chloe said, her tone filled with awe. Her gaze traveled over the huge elephant with its wrinkled gray skin and ivory tusk, the zebra with its distinctive black and white stripes, and the lion with its razor-sharp teeth. She leaned across the rope to get closer. "They appear alive. I want to reach out and pet the zebra."

The look of wonder on her lovely face was genuine, and

Michael found it hard to tear his gaze away. Her breathing was rapid and her breasts rose and fell temptingly against the neckline of her gown. Her blue eyes shone with excitement and eagerness. He felt the stirrings of desire, and annoyance rose within him.

Bloody hell. He was here to protect Henry from her scheming, not lust after the chit. But something about Chloe Somerton was exotic as well. Just like the animals behind the rope, she possessed a rare, wild beauty.

Mr. Bullock prodded them onward. "Come along. There's much more to see."

The group toured rooms with historical arms and armor as well as a room with more Egyptian rarities, including a sarcophagus. Michael stayed a step behind the group, where he could observe Chloe and Henry. The pair chatted about the displays. Anyone who saw her would swear she was a proper lady. Her gown was of the highest quality, her posture straight, and even the movements of her hands were elegant and graceful in her gloves. A picture arose in his mind of her nimble fingers slipping inside a man's waistcoat. The vision was arousing and infuriating at once.

He had to do something about this, but what? He had no intention of telling young Henry the truth. He'd have to deal with the lying lady on his own.

"Miss Chloe," Henry said, interrupting Michael's thoughts. "Since you've recently returned from Hampshire, would you like to see more of London? Hyde Park is lovely this time of year. I'd be honored to take you for a ride in my barouche." Henry glanced at Lady Huntingdon. "With your sister's approval, of course."

A blush tinged Chloe's cheeks. "A ride in the park sounds wonderful."

Michael gritted his teeth. He didn't like this turn of events. They had barely been in the museum for an hour and already

Henry was making plans with her. At this rate, the reading of the banns would be arranged before they left the damned museum.

Mr. Bullock's heels clicked on the marble floor as he led the group. "The next room holds a special surprise."

They found themselves back in the corridor, following their guide until they came to another arched doorway. Mr. Bullock opened a door and motioned for the group to enter.

Michael was the last one inside, his narrowed gaze intently focused on Henry and Chloe. Henry lowered his head to speak in Chloe's ear and she laughed. Not an annoying, high-pitched giggle of the sort he'd heard from many debutantes at the countless balls he'd been obligated to attend since his brother's and father's deaths, but a rich, throaty laugh. His skin heated at the sound.

"Look!" Lady Huntingdon said.

Michael's attention snapped to his surroundings. The room was empty save for a large carriage that sat upon a wooden dais. He stopped short as his gaze homed in on the distinctive Imperial Arms emblazoned on the paneled door.

It can't be...

His jaw stiffened. "What—"

"It's Napoleon's private traveling carriage captured by the Prussian Major von Keller as Napoleon fled the Battle of Waterloo." Mr. Bullock's voice rose an octave. He motioned to the dark blue conveyance embellished with gold frieze.

"Fascinating! May we sit inside?" Lady Huntingdon asked.

All at once, the group chattered excitedly as they approached the carriage.

Michael stiffened as a low buzzing started in his ears. His vision tunneled to pinpoints of light, the gilded edges of the crest on the door shimmering into a thousand shards. He wavered on his feet, then reached out for the doorjamb for support. The walls felt as if they were closing in like the bars of a prison. Despite every ounce of effort, his temperature swiftly began to rise and sweat beaded on his brow.

Christ, not here.

Not now.

He fought the panic. Fought the escalating rise of his heartbeat and the icy fear that clawed at his innards, but he knew he would fail. He watched as the group circled the golden carriage. Henry opened the door, and Lady Huntingdon stepped inside. Her laugh echoed and rattled inside his skull. He watched, his body immobile, as she reached out to shut the carriage door. The click of the latch sounded as loud as a gunshot, and he jerked.

Voices vaguely registered through a tunnel in his brain.

"Thousands of visitors have come to see it," Mr. Bullock said. "Napoleon himself approved the design. It's rumored to resist bullets."

"It was initially sent as a present to the Prince Regent," Henry said.

"The spacious interior can be adapted to a bedroom, dressing room, and even an eating room," Mr. Bullock spoke again.

Michael sagged against the doorframe. He had to leave. Extract himself. But his hessians felt filled with lead, and his body failed to cooperate. His gaze was riveted on the curve of the crest, the shining gold facets of the carriage.

The last time he'd seen the conveyance, amid smoke and deafening cannon fire, bodies had littered the battlefield, and he'd cradled his friend's lifeless body in his arms.

Get out. Now.

With sheer force of will, he staggered out of the room and leaned heavily against the outside wall. Breathing deeply, he clenched and unclenched his fists and counted. He reached one hundred and eight before his vision returned to normal and the panic began to dissipate.

He pulled a handkerchief from his coat pocket and wiped his damp brow. He wandered aimlessly down the hall and paced back and forth until his heartbeat slowed and his body temperature returned to normal.

He'd lost track of time. Had it been ten or twenty minutes since he'd left? He could hear voices. The group was still enjoying Napoleon's carriage and they were asking to take turns sitting on the plush, red velvet cushions. He straightened and reached up to ensure his cravat was in place. He could do this. He could return and no one would be the wiser.

Still, he hated that he'd been completely helpless to prevent the episode, and anger and frustration roiled in his gut at his weakness. The triggers were different each time, but the fits were always the same, sudden and shocking, throwing him off balance and sending him back to past events, shadowy and gruesome battlefields that he wanted to forget. How long would this last? He'd been home for months and the fits continued—even seemed to worsen. Was this his fate? To become the mad duke?

No. He owed his friend and he had a duty to carry out.

He returned to stand outside the room. Taking one more deep breath, he took a step forward and collided with Chloe Somerton.

"Oh!" she cried out, stumbling back.

Instinctively, he reached out to grasp her arms.

Her blue eyes widened. "Pardon, Your Grace. I didn't see you."

Up close, she was even more striking. The top of her head reached his shoulder, and she tipped her face up to look at him. Her skin was flawless and smooth, and her blue eyes were fringed with thick lashes. The scent of lemongrass filled his nostrils. Fresh and pure.

He understood how Henry was besotted.

"I'm fine now. You can let go," she said.

He realized he was staring. His fingers flexed and he reluctantly released his hold.

A tiny crease formed between her brows. "Are you well, Your Grace?"

Of course she could tell something was wrong with him. One fraud could recognize another.

"I know who you are," he said, his voice terse.

A finely arched eyebrow shot up. "Pardon?"

"I know about your past. I'm responsible for Henry. His father died on the battlefield under my command, you see. I swore to look after his son, and I intend to honor that promise."

She tilted her head to the side and regarded him. "If you're referring to my family's history then you needn't bother. Henry is aware that my father was the infamous art forger who duped half of the *ton*. Henry knows and is unfazed."

His lips thinned into a grim line. "Your family's history is damning enough, but that's not what I'm referring to."

"Then what?"

He leaned close and gave her his sternest no-nonsense stare, one that made battle-hardened soldiers snap to attention and quiver in their boots. "You're a thief, Chloe Somerton. A pickpocket, to be precise. And you're as far from a lady as one can imagine."

She stiffened, but to his astonishment, she didn't cower or flinch. Not one tear glimmered in her lovely blue eyes. Rather, she lifted her chin and met his icy gaze.

"So? What do you want?"

He blinked. "It's simple. Stay away from Henry."

Full pink lips curled in a slow, mocking smile. "Not a chance, Your Grace."

• • •

He knows!

As Chloe Somerton returned to the room, her face was serene, her steps measured and graceful. Inwardly, her heart was pounding as loud as a drum in her chest. She tightened her fingers in her skirts so that no one would notice them trembling.

She was furious. Furious and fearful—a volatile combination.

Henry approached her. "What do you like best of Napoleon's carriage?"

Chloe gifted him with an innocent smile. "It's a beautiful piece. The Imperial Arms emblazoned on the panels of the doors are lovely, of course, but it's the smaller details I find truly fascinating. The lamps on each corner of the roof, combined with the one in the back, can cleverly illuminate the interior. They can even be used to heat food."

He leaned close to whisper. "Fascinating. Most would focus on the ornamentation and not appreciate the design of the conveyance."

Her smile brightened like she hadn't a care in the world. She liked Henry. He was young, just twenty-two and close to her age of near twenty. He was also handsome with brown hair and eyes and a lithe build.

Chloe's instincts told her that Henry, the Earl of Sefton, would make a wonderful husband. He was kind, attentive, and charming.

He was also rich and titled.

Just perfect.

She stole a glimpse at the tall and grimly unsmiling man in the back of the room.

Heavens.

There was nothing kind or considerate about the Duke of Cameron. Dark, arrogant, and dangerous were only a few words a lady could use to describe him. He was also arrestingly handsome. The meticulously tailored jacket emphasized broad shoulders and a muscular physique. He was well over six feet in height, and his dark hair gleamed from a ray of sunlight from one of the museum's windows. His profile was chiseled, as if an artist had selected the finest marble before carving his model. His eyes were dark as midnight. He was clearly a man in his prime, but the duke's commanding presence made him appear older.

He turned, fully revealing his face, and she sucked in a breath. She knew he'd been a military man, a lieutenant colonel in the king's army. It made perfect sense. He had a resolute strength about him and he carried himself like an officer, like a man used to having his commands followed. Her face heated as she thought of how she'd walked into him just outside the room. The hardness of his chest—it was like a solid wall of muscle. His body was evidence of hard labor—a warriors' body, certainly not a duke's.

She shivered despite the warmth in the room. She could not believe it. The Duke of Cameron knew her secret. How was it possible? Of all the gentlemen in the *beau monde*, why did he have to take an interest in Henry?

It wasn't his size or the coiled power in his muscular frame that had sent a shiver down her spine, but the fierce look in his eyes. He'd looked like he was about to set foot on the battlefield. Determined yet unfocused. He'd been sweating…uneasy…almost as if he'd been in *pain*. His grip on her shoulders had tightened, and he'd shocked her by calling her a thief.

He'd been right. She had picked pockets years ago, had stolen in order to survive poverty. But her sins hadn't ceased at mere thievery.

Just how much *did* he know? She could only hope his knowledge wasn't complete. Even her two older sisters were ignorant of the truth…

Sweet Lord. The knowledge was a weapon in anyone's hands, let alone the duke's.

Anger and fear shifted swiftly into other all too familiar feelings—remorse and regret. It didn't matter that she'd acted to survive; the shame would never entirely go away.

She swallowed hard. There was only one possible course of action.

She had to see the duke in private. Plead her case. The duke hadn't told Henry, that much she was certain. The adoration on Henry' face as he gazed at her surely would evaporate if he knew of her past.

All of her past.

She stole another glimpse over her shoulder to find the Duke of Cameron watching her. Leaning against the wall, his arms were folded across his broad chest. He caught her staring and a dark eyebrow rose in challenge.

He had the power to ruin everything.

Chapter Two

Chloe pulled the hood of her cloak over her head and stared at the imposing mansion in Berkeley Square. She'd paid the hackney driver to wait for her around the corner. A full moon illuminated the massive pile of stone. The structure was even larger than her brother-in-law Huntingdon's home, and she couldn't imagine one person occupying such a large residence.

She took a breath and climbed the steps to reach for the brass knocker. Banging twice, she stepped back and waited. The door swung open to reveal a stern-faced butler with military bearing. His hard eyes swept her from head to toe then returned to her face.

Straightening her spine, she met the servant's unfriendly glare. "I'm here to see His Grace."

"Whom may I say is calling at this hour?"

"Kindly inform him that Miss Chloe Somerton would like to speak with him."

The servant looked at her in disdain, and she could only imagine the thoughts that were running through his head. A lady of quality never visited a bachelor's home without a proper chaperone, let alone late at night. Did he assume she was here for a secret liaison?

She raised her chin a notch. "I assure you, he'll want to see me. It is a most important matter."

The butler smirked. Once again, she wondered if he believed her to be the duke's lover. She should be ashamed, but desperation pushed aside the unwelcome feelings. He opened the door wide. "Step inside, and I shall tell His Grace that he has a visitor."

Chloe sighed with relief. Lowering her hood, she took in her surroundings. Marble pillars and a marble floor graced a magnificent vestibule. A winding staircase with an elaborate gilded balustrade led up to a second floor. Priceless artwork hung on the walls and a Chinese vase full of colorful blooms sat on a dainty Chippendale table, filling the space with a heady perfume. As a girl who'd spent time in the slums, she still appreciated such wealth. Her nervousness returned in earnest.

Before the butler could take her cloak, footsteps echoed off the marble floor and Cameron himself appeared in the vestibule.

Oh my.

He was even more striking than she'd remembered, and he was having the same effect on her as when she'd first seen him in the museum. The duke's classical features possessed a primitive appeal. His hair was inky black, and he wore it long enough to brush his collar. She'd never before seen hair that dark, and it brought forth images of pirates, raiders, and other dangerous villains. His eyes held an unmistakable sheen of intelligence, and there was an air of isolation in his tall figure, as if he knew his place in the world, and he carried himself with the utmost confidence. An impressive man, powerfully masculine. The type of male that caused women to act foolishly.

He was without jacket or cravat, in his shirtsleeves, trousers, and hessians. He held a sheaf of papers, and she realized he must have been working.

His piercing gaze raked her form before returning to her face. "Well…well," he drawled. "Miss Somerton. What a pleasant surprise." His tone suggested it wasn't a surprise at all and that he'd been expecting her to arrive late at night on his doorstep.

Impossible.

Chloe's heart pounded in her chest as she was held captive by his dark gaze. "May we speak in private, Your Grace?"

"You are alone? No chaperone?"

She swallowed. "I thought it best this way."

His lips quirked. "Yes. I believe we have something important to discuss that requires the utmost privacy." He motioned toward the hallway leading from the vestibule. "We can talk in my library. Shall we?"

For a brief moment, her nerves almost faltered, and she clutched her reticule before her.

One dark brow shot upward. "Come now, Miss Somerton. You haven't sneaked out of your home unchaperoned to visit a bachelor's residence only to lose your nerve now, have you?"

"Of course not," she snapped.

She stepped forward and followed as he led her down the hall. She stole a sidelong glance at the clear-cut lines of his profile.

He stopped outside a door, held it open for her, and motioned for her to enter. She swept inside the duke's private library and halted. The room was paneled in rich mahogany, and row after row of bookshelves lined the walls. Supple leather spines of different colors occupied every inch of the shelves. Chloe knew how costly books were, and she suspected one of the leather-bound volumes could have paid their rent at the print shop for a month. A pair of matching leather chairs was situated beside a large fireplace with a coal brazier and a marble mantle. She could picture herself sitting in one of the chairs, her legs curled beneath her, as she read for hours.

As she walked farther into the room, her eye was drawn to a large rack of rolled parchments in the corner. One was unrolled across a six-foot-long desk to reveal an extensive map of Europe with markings. It looked like a battle plan, and she remembered that the Duke of Cameron had been a military man.

She recalled what little she'd learned about him from her sister on the carriage ride home from Bullock's Museum. Eliza tended to chatter about people and events, and she had been excited that a duke had accompanied them during the museum tour. Chloe had wanted to unearth as much information as she could, but at the same time, she'd been careful not to question Eliza and arouse her suspicions. The duke was a second son. Chloe thought it ironic that he'd returned from war alive and physically uninjured while his father and older brother had died in a carriage accident in the London streets. He'd unexpectedly and tragically inherited the dukedom.

"May I take your cloak?" His fingers brushed her shoulders, sending a shiver of awareness through her at the slight contact as he removed her cloak and placed it on a settee tucked in the corner of the library.

He motioned to the leather chairs before the fireplace. "Please sit." It was a command more than a request. She suspected he was used to issuing orders and others obeying. She didn't see any reason to ignore him, so she settled in the chair and smoothed her skirts.

"Would you like a drink? I was about to pour myself one before you arrived."

Strong spirits could only help her nerves. "Yes, thank

you."

He walked to a cabinet and withdrew a crystal decanter of amber-colored alcohol. He poured a finger's worth in one crystal glass, offering it to her, then filled the second glass halfway. He sat in the leather chair across from her and stretched out his long legs. Lamplight glinted off his polished hessians, and his trousers hugged his muscular legs. Her gaze was drawn to the V at his throat where the top two buttons of his shirt were undone. A sprinkling of hair and tanned skin drew her eye.

Did he ride without a jacket and cravat? The image sent her pulse racing.

She lifted the drink to her lips. The first gulp burned her throat and every inch of her esophagus on the way down to her stomach, and she coughed. "What is this?" she rasped.

His perfect mouth curved in a smile as he raised his glass. "Fine scotch whisky. The second sip will go down easier." He leaned forward and rested his hand on his knee. "Now, to what do I owe this pleasure?"

She took a breath and met his gaze. "I'm here to discuss what happened at the museum this afternoon."

"Ah, I see."

He sipped his drink. Not wanting to appear cowardly, she followed suit. He was right. The second taste went a bit easier. The alcohol warmed her blood, eased her nerves, and increased her courage a notch. "I prefer to handle difficulties directly," she said.

"Of course, you do. You handled things quite directly the first time I saw you. If my memory is accurate, you were filching embroidered handkerchiefs from men's coats."

She sat still, afraid to breathe.

This was what she'd feared. How did he know, dammit?

She mentally debated lying or bursting into female hysterics, but she instinctively knew those tricks wouldn't work on him.

She raised her chin and pushed her shoulders back, bold as brass. "I have no idea what you are talking about. I would never bother with simple handkerchiefs when I could lift a fat purse just as easily."

A moment of frigid silence passed, then he threw his head back and laughed richly. She was taken aback by his reaction, and her eyes were riveted to the corded muscles of his throat.

"Bravo! I expected a simpering miss and an adamant denial." He leaned forward, his broad shoulders straining against the fabric of his shirt. Her gaze snapped back to his face and her unease returned in earnest. His humor didn't quite reach those icy dark eyes.

"I know about your past," he said. "Your father was Jonathan Miller, the infamous art forger of the *ton*, who fleeced many, then abandoned his three daughters rather than face imprisonment. Thereafter, you opened the Peacock Print Shop to survive. You were all shopkeepers."

"It's no longer a secret." Their father's crimes had left them destitute and desperate. If it were not for Eliza's business sense and for Amelia's talent with a paintbrush, they would still be in a St. Giles rookery. Both the Earls of Huntingdon and Vale knew, and neither had cared, when they married her sisters. Their pasts were forgotten. At least her sisters' pasts.

Chloe's past was a bit different.

"You are the youngest, correct? I assume you tired of working the long hours of a shopkeeper and thought to supplement your income by thievery."

Clenching her teeth, her temper flared. "You know nothing, Your Grace," she snapped. Of course, he would think the worst of her. A man in his position had never known hardship.

"I know enough," he said, his voice low but dangerous.

"Henry…I mean, Lord Sefton looks up to you. He

idolizes you."

The duke's expression was grim. "I owe his father my life. I won't let him be fooled by a fortune-scheming miss."

The barb hurt, like salt on an open wound. Why did the duke have to be Henry's self-appointed 'guardian'? Why couldn't it have been anyone else?

She buried the bitterness his accusation stirred in her heart and tried to reason with him. "How can I assure you that my past is long forgotten? We have all started a new life. I have no intention of hurting Henry. I truly like him."

"You like him?" His expression was mocking.

Her stomach fluttered at the coldness in the duke's eyes. "Yes."

"Then send him away. Discourage his interest. Set your feminine trap for another unsuspecting man."

Another surge of anger made her breath burn in her throat. Who was he to pass such quick judgment? A man born in luxury, an aristocrat whose place in the *ton* was guaranteed from the day of his birth, a *duke* who was one step below royalty.

He'd never known hunger or cold or prolonged illness because he couldn't afford medicine from the apothecary or care from a physician.

She pushed a wayward tendril of hair away from her cheek. His eyes followed her movements, making her uneasy. "I won't be bullied. Both Huntingdon and Vale will protect me."

She was bluffing. Her sisters didn't know of her past exploits to get the money they'd so desperately needed, and she had no intention of telling them. Her brothers-in-law had no idea, either. It was a secret she planned to take to her grave.

The duke's knowledge of her past was her weakness. A chink in her armor.

Sipping his drink, he leaned back in his chair, a confident

expression on his handsome face. "Then you will force me to reveal the truth about your past. The *entire* truth. Would you put your family through such a trial when all you have to do to protect them is discourage one suitor?"

She met his hard eyes without flinching. She refused to be bullied by him. She was a fighter. A survivor. "I won't do it. And you shall keep my secret."

His eyes flashed. "Oh? Why is that?"

"Because Henry has already suffered from the death of his father. Telling him my past will only cause him further undue distress." She might be uncertain about how far the duke would go to ruin her, but she knew he'd promised Henry's father that he would look after his son. If she were lucky, that responsibility would extend to Henry's emotional well-being.

Cameron's eyes narrowed, and he lowered his glass. "A worthy opponent. You fascinate me, Chloe Somerton."

"You make it sound as if you are never challenged."

"Challenged, yes. Defeated, never." He took her empty glass from her and set it aside on an end table, then brushed the backs of his fingers over her cheek. "Still, I admire your spirit. You must know you're a beautiful woman, and I suspect you are accustomed to using everything to your advantage."

She gasped at his touch, and her awareness of him heightened. Her thoughts spun at his smoldering gaze. He thought her beautiful? She knew her fair looks and blue eyes attracted men, but to hear it from *him* made her shiver.

"You're blushing, Miss Somerton."

She touched her heated cheek, and her lips parted with a scathing retort, but he raised his hand before she could speak.

"But it's not your looks that draw my attention," he said. "It's rare to find someone who isn't intimidated by me, either as a duke or as a military man. You are a rare exception."

Trapped by the intensity of his stare as much as by his

words, her heart stuttered in her chest. "Forgive me if I find your words not as complimentary as you think they should be."

His lips twisted in a cynical smile. "Exactly my point. You have spirit, and I like a challenge."

What on earth was he saying? She nervously nibbled her bottom lip, and his eyes dropped to her mouth. She felt an undeniable tug of attraction.

Ridiculous. She hated the man.

"How much will it take, then?" he said.

Her brow furrowed. "Pardon?"

"How much? Five hundred pounds…a thousand? I'm a wealthy man. Name your price."

She sucked in a breath as realization struck. "You think to pay me to stay away from Henry?"

"You are an astute woman," he drawled.

"You're jesting."

"I never jest."

She rose to her feet and smoothed her skirts. He immediately stood. "I shall see myself out," she said.

She turned, but his hand snaked out to grasp her wrist. "Not yet."

Her eyes widened at the contact. His hands were calloused, his tapered fingers firm. A warrior's hands. She experienced a shiver of apprehension and, heaven help her, excitement, from the leashed strength in him, the mysterious depth of his eyes, and the warmth of his skin.

"Sit," he said. "We have not finished our business."

Chapter Three

The touch of Michael's fingers on the slender bones of Chloe's wrist sent a jolt of lust to his brain. Her breathing was rapid, and her breasts rose and fell temptingly against the neckline of her gown. Her full lips parted, and he knew she felt the undeniable attraction as well.

Chloe yanked her wrist away, and he reluctantly released her. "I don't want your money or anything you have to offer," she said coolly. "As you've already observed, I'm not like most women."

No, she wasn't. She was infinitely more interesting.

He sipped his whisky, savoring the expensive alcohol as much as the woman seated across from him. Despite what he'd said earlier, he was surprised by Chloe Somerton's unchaperoned, late-night visit. He was rarely surprised by people's behavior. One of the things he'd learned as a military officer was to study the patterns of his enemies and attempt to predict their next move. He'd become good at it, and other officers looked to him for strategy and planning. People were no different. Until Chloe Somerton had reappeared.

She was unpredictable.

He tamped down his desire. He needed to have his wits about him. He could not allow Chloe Somerton, no matter how attractive, to distract him from his purpose. He owed a debt of honor that he intended to uphold.

Her fingers twisted in her lap. "Your attempts at bribery are for naught. I won't hurt Henry."

"You are a thief and a liar. Forgive me if I don't believe a word you say."

Her blue eyes sparked with fury. "Do you want to know what I think?"

He leaned back in his seat. "Please enlighten me."

"You're bluffing. You attempted to use your dukedom, your wealth, and even your physical presence to intimidate and bribe me. You have failed on every account."

It was as if she'd thrown down a gauntlet. The months since the war had been mundane. He'd joined the army and purchased his commission as a younger son, a spare. But he'd returned from battle only to learn that his father and brother had died in a freak accident, and he was the new Duke of Cameron. He'd had his fair share of difficulty managing all the estates, but it hadn't been close to the flash of challenge in her eyes.

"As I said, I believe telling Henry my past would devastate him," she said.

Devastate him, *not her*. Her words revealed the true extent of her emotions regarding his young ward. She knew Henry would be horribly upset if Michael revealed Chloe's past and ruined her reputation. Henry could never propose to her. She would suffer the consequences of scandal, but she wouldn't be heartbroken, which confirmed she didn't love Henry.

Why did that thought buoy him? He must be a heartless bastard after all.

"You need a man, Chloe Somerton, not a boy."

"You think Henry is a boy and that I need someone else?"

"That's precisely what I mean."

"I see. And you think it should be you?"

"Why not?" The thought came to him suddenly and the words were out of his lips before he could consider all the consequences. Since his return to England, he hadn't bothered with a mistress. Even that type of relationship seemed too permanent. He enjoyed women, of course, but only brief affairs with widows who'd wanted a night of pleasure in his bed, never innocent, unmarried ladies.

Which made him wonder if she was even a virgin. She wasn't raised in a proper household. Her father had been a thief and a criminal. And if she had been immoral enough to follow his example and steal, then it wasn't a far leap to assume that she'd been with a man. Either way, there was something about Chloe Somerton that provoked and aroused him.

Once again, she stood abruptly, and he followed. But instead of reaching for her cloak and attempting to flee, a coy look crossed her face and she licked those pink lips. Reaching out, she touched him with the tip of her forefinger to the center of his chest. She grazed his shirt, just above his heart, and he sucked in a breath. Every inch of his skin tightened in awareness.

Jesus.

"Careful, my lady. You play with fire." His voice was hoarse to his own ears.

She dropped her hand and a satisfied smile curled her lips. "You're wrong," she said in a taunting voice. "You are the last type of man I want or need."

"Prove it," he said.

She hesitated. "How?"

"A kiss. If you don't feel anything, then I'll believe you

have true feelings for young Henry."

"I cannot."

"What are you afraid of? I'll keep your secret and leave you to enjoy Henry's pursuit."

He could see the indecision in her eyes. He was surprised at how badly he wanted her to agree, to take the challenge. At last, her impulsive nature won and she took a step forward. "All right. One kiss." Standing on tiptoe, she clutched her hands by her sides, raised her pert chin, and shut her eyes.

His lips twitched with humor as he gazed down at her upturned face. Seconds passed, then she opened her eyes. "Well?"

"I prefer you to look at me."

"And I prefer to shut—"

He pulled her to him and swooped down to capture her mouth. Desire spiraled in his gut at the very first touch of their lips. Her hands were against his chest, but she didn't push him away. She wasn't as tall as he liked, but her lush curves pressed against his hard angles in all the right places. She tasted like wild strawberries and the whisky he should not have given her. It was a tantalizing combination and reminded him just how complicated the lady was. He felt his iron control slip, and he caressed the length of her back and pressed closer.

She gasped, and he took advantage and his tongue swept inside her mouth. Her fingers curled into the linen fabric of his shirt, and her lips relaxed beneath his. The tentative stroke of her tongue, hesitant and light as a butterfly, tangled with his. An explosion of lust shot straight to his groin. Instinct took over and he increased the pressure of his kiss, his tongue greedily exploring the recesses of her mouth.

The uneven rhythm of her breathing made him come to his senses. This had gone too far and was not what he'd intended. With effort, he lifted his head to gaze down at her upturned face.

His voice was hoarse. "Just as I thought. There's fierce passion in you, Chloe Somerton. Don't waste it on a boy."

She touched her lips. "You're wrong. I felt nothing."

"Little liar. Your body trembled at the first touch of my lips. And even if you were as frigid as a block of ice, I would still insist you leave Lord Sefton be."

"You may be a duke, but you are *not* a gentleman."

"There's no room for chivalry in war."

"And is this war?"

"Only if you don't obey."

Blue sparks flashed in her eyes. "So be it, Your Grace." Whirling away, she snatched her cloak from the settee and walked out of the room with a swirl of skirts. He heard her footsteps down the marble hall, and a moment later, the front door slammed closed.

Michael followed Chloe at a discreet distance until he saw her climb into a hackney at the end of the street. At least she had the good sense to tell the driver to wait. He imagined her slipping through the servants' entrance at Huntingdon's home, or knowing her audacity, she may attempt to climb through one of the windows.

He curled his lips into a smile. He wouldn't put anything past Chloe Somerton.

Michael returned to the library, poured himself another whisky, sat in the chair, and stretched his booted feet before him. Sleep would elude him tonight, as it did almost every night since he'd returned from the war. A memory of his friend, Sefton, rose before him, and Michael absentmindedly rubbed the thin scar beneath his chin. They'd met as homesick boys at Eaton and had disliked each other at first until Michael had defended twelve-year-old Sefton from the school tyrant. Michael had won the fight, but he'd received the scar. Thereafter, Sefton and Michael had become best friends, and they'd gone on to Oxford before joining the army.

Michael sighed. He sipped his drink, savoring the expensive alcohol, hoping it would numb him enough to get a few hours respite.

His thoughts returned to the lady.

He picked up her discarded glass on the end table, and lamplight flickered off the cut crystal. He envied the glass where her lips touched. He envisioned her full pink lips parting for his kiss, the smooth, expensive whisky on her tongue.

The possession of her mouth had nearly brought him to his knees. He hadn't expected the flare of lust from one simple kiss.

Had he been wrong about her? Could she be sexually innocent?

Highly unlikely.

He'd seen her pick pockets with quick, skillful fingers. She was a consummate actress and skilled at deception and thievery.

He'd first seen her on Bond Street when he'd accompanied his brother, Everet, on the way to the shoemaker's for a new pair of boots. Everet had spotted a friend from Oxford and had stopped to speak with the man. Michael had waited nearby as pedestrians entered shops and wandered along the busy street. Couples chatted, and a hawker selling fresh baked rolls called out, selling his wares outside a bakery. It was a pleasant spring afternoon, and people were out enjoying the fine weather and the wares of the London shops.

Then he saw her.

Her pale hair was pulled back in a bun and she wore a faded blue dress. Her clothing was simple, certainly not that of a wealthy lady but of the working class. A shopkeeper, most likely. She was smiling and the sun glinted off her golden hair, and when she turned to face him he was struck by a pair of the bluest eyes he'd ever seen. She was charming. Lovely.

And young.

She was carrying a basket with what looked like cakes of paint and brushes. An artist? His gaze followed her as she wove through the crowd. He noticed she was following a pair of dandies, gentlemen with flowered waistcoats, ridiculously high-pointed collars, and beaver hats. The men were strutting about like arrogant peacocks, reveling in the attention from the passersby. The lady kept two or three paces behind them. Subtle, very subtle. Anyone else watching would never have thought she was following the pair, but Michael was a military man, and he knew a well-practiced maneuver when he spotted one.

Then she bumped into one of the dandies, blushed prettily, and anyone watching would think that was the end of it. But sure enough, her slender fingers snuck into a flowered waistcoat and pulled out a handkerchief. With a flick of her wrist, the stolen good was tucked into her basket. He watched, absorbed, as she efficiently pilfered three more items from well-dressed gentlemen. Two additional handkerchiefs and a snuffbox.

Damn, she was good.

Then Everet had called his name, distracting Michael. An instant later, he had turned back, but she had disappeared into the crowd.

Fascinating.

He'd never attempted to summon a constable. From the look of the dandy's fine clothing, when he discovered his handkerchief missing, he would think he dropped it in the street or forgotten it at home in a chest of drawers cluttered with dozens of similar handkerchiefs. Either way, it would be no hardship to the man's purse.

The other men looked just as wealthy. Michael had felt a stab of sympathy for the bloke who had his snuffbox taken, but for some reason, he had not notified the man or the authorities. Something about the girl was compelling, enchanting, and he hadn't wanted to see her shackled and dragged away by a hardened, unsympathetic constable.

Michael had thought of the lady thief for days afterward. He'd returned to the same spot on Bond Street several times over the next two weeks, hoping to spot her, but she'd never appeared. She'd slipped through his fingers then, only to show up now, five years later.

Chloe's life circumstances may have changed, but her unscrupulous past remained a part of her. Instead of filching handkerchiefs or other belongings from wealthy men, she planned to snag the young Earl of Sefton and his fortune.

Not on my watch, she won't.

He grinned as he sipped his whisky. He hadn't cared about anything in a long, long time. His evenings were filled with dread as he recalled the final battle and the sacrifice of his best friend—the sacrifice that had ensured Michael's return home, and Henry's father's—the former Earl of Sefton's—funeral.

But now, for the first time in over a year, Michael's thoughts were occupied by the lady's unexpected visit and the challenge shining in her exquisite sapphire eyes. He may not have planned on kissing her, but he didn't regret it.

Chapter Four

The night had been a disaster.

Chloe entered the servants' entrance of Huntingdon's town house and slipped up the stairs into her bedchamber. Her trusted maid, Alice, was sitting on the edge of the four-poster waiting for her.

Alice jumped to her feet as soon as Chloe shut the door. "Thank heavens! What took you so long?"

"I was delayed. Did anyone suspect I left the house?"

"Not a soul. Your sister and Lord Huntingdon believe you went to bed early with a headache." Alice placed a nightgown on the bed and set to work unfastening the buttons on the back of Chloe's dress. "What did the duke say?"

Chloe took a breath. "He believes I'm a fraud. He warned me to stay away from Henry."

Alice's fingers stilled on the buttons. "Lord!"

Alice was near Chloe's age. She had been born and raised in the rookeries, and Chloe had met her when she and her sisters had no choice but to stay in St. Giles after their father's abandonment. Only Chloe knew that Alice had worked in the

Seven Sins brothel, not as a prostitute, but as a kitchen maid. No matter how open-minded Eliza was regarding aiding the servants, Chloe didn't think she would agree to keep Alice on if she knew the full truth.

Her maid brushed a stray lock of brown hair from her cap. "Did he say anything else?"

Chloe shook her head. She'd never confess the duke had done more than speak with her. His unexpected kiss had unsettled her more than she liked to admit, and she needed time alone to think.

"What will you do?" Alice helped Chloe step out of the dress and then began to untie her stays.

Once her corset was removed, Chloe took a deep breath and slipped into her nightgown. "Nothing. I don't think the duke will say anything. Cameron wouldn't want to upset Henry so soon after the death of his father."

"Even if the duke tells Lord Sefton that you picked pockets, you should feel no guilt. You chose to survive. There is no fault in that. You are a good woman, Chloe Somerton. If it wasn't for your kindness and compassion, I'd be rotting in a St. Giles's alley by now."

Tears stung Chloe's eyes, and she embraced Alice. "Thank you, Alice."

"Now. None of that. Get into bed," Alice said as she pulled back the covers to tuck Chloe in for the night. She extinguished the lamp, then opened the door. "Sweet dreams, Miss Chloe."

In the dark solitude of her room, Chloe thought about her maid's words.

Kind. Compassionate. Good.

She felt a nauseating despair. She wasn't so sure Alice was right. After all, Jonathan Miller's tainted blood ran through her veins.

Soon her thoughts turned to the duke, and she tossed and

turned in bed as vivid memories of the battle-hardened man returned in a rush. She'd visited Cameron's mansion because she had been hoping to reason with him, to admit to her past misdeeds, and assure him that she hadn't participated in any illegal activities in years. She'd embarked on a new life long ago. She had no intention of hurting Henry or reverting to her old ways. But the duke refused to believe her.

In his mind, she was a criminal—no better than her own father.

Maybe he's right.

Her stomach tilted. All she wanted was what countless debutantes at Almack's desired and what her own sisters had obtained. A title. Wealth. A wedding band.

Security.

But fate had dealt her a different hand of cards. Her sins were different from her sisters'. Worse. It didn't matter how much they had needed funds in the past. It didn't matter that they'd been desperate because of her—because she'd been sick. She had taken her crimes a step...or several steps... further than Eliza and Amelia.

Her heart fluttered behind her breast. Instead of reasoning with the duke, she was now in a precarious position. And then he'd *kissed* her.

Never in her wildest dreams had she thought the press of his hard lips against hers would make her heart leap. The unexpected sizzling heat was as dangerous as it was unwanted. For a brief moment, the rest of the world didn't exist, just the arousing caress of his kiss. Tingles had rushed through her and swept over her skin. Only a faint voice of reason kept her from clinging to his broad shoulders and pressing against his hard body.

What had come over her?

He was dangerous. Not only did she feel a sweeping pull low in her stomach when he touched her, but he knew part of her deepest secrets. And he'd threatened to reveal them.

Bloody hell. Sleep would be elusive tonight.

. . .

The following morning, Chloe was still tired as she descended the grand staircase. Images of constables chasing her through the city streets had haunted her dreams. The nightmare wasn't unusual but—for the first time—it had changed last night. The constable's face took on the darkly handsome image of the Duke of Cameron. She'd woken, heart pounding, a sheen of perspiration on her forehead. It had taken several minutes for the vision to fade and reality to return.

She yawned as her foot landed on the last step. Her nose twitched as the smell of coffee wafted to her. *Thank the Lord.*

She hurried to the breakfast room to find Eliza sitting at the table, a steaming plate of eggs before her, sipping a cup of coffee. Chloe glanced at a long sideboard holding chafing dishes of eggs, bacon, and rolls. Her stomach growled.

"Good grief, Chloe. You have dark circles beneath your eyes and you look like you haven't slept in days." Eliza set her cup on her saucer and stared at her sister.

"Good morning to you, too," Chloe said.

"Are you well? Has your headache subsided?" Eliza's brow furrowed in concern.

Most of the annoyance fled from Chloe at her sister's look of concern. Chloe's stomach dropped, and she knew Eliza worried she was ill.

Chloe smoothed her hair. "I'm fine. I just had trouble sleeping."

"Again? Perhaps you should have Alice bring you a cup of warm milk tonight before you retire."

"I'll be sure to ask her." Chloe doubted drinking warm milk would have helped her last night.

She picked up a plate and started filling it with poached eggs and bacon from the sideboard, then joined her sister at the table and spread her napkin on her lap. "Where's Huntingdon?"

"He had an appointment. A new artist has a showing," Eliza said.

Huntingdon was a renowned art critic. He'd also been fooled by their father, Jonathan Miller, the talented forger, years ago. But fate had been kind to the three sisters, and instead of seeking revenge against their father, Lord Huntingdon had fallen madly in love with Eliza and married her.

A liveried footman entered the breakfast room with a pot of coffee, and Chloe nearly wept with joy. "Thank you," she said as the servant poured her cup.

Chloe picked up her fork just as the butler came forth carrying a silver salver. "These just arrived for you, my lady."

Eliza took two letters and broke a red seal on the first one. "Why, it's from Huntingdon's aunt, Lady Holand, in Scotland. She must be in her mideighties. She needs a companion and wonders if I know a suitable young lady."

Chloe sipped her coffee. "Doesn't she live in the wilds of Scotland? That may be difficult."

"Yes, but I will make inquiries for her."

Eliza reached for the second letter and her face lit. "It's from Amelia. She and Lord Vale plan to return from Hampshire next week."

Chloe's mood turned buoyant, and she smiled. "I know it has only been a month, but I miss her terribly." Their middle sister, Amelia, had recently married the Earl of Vale and they'd been away at their Hampshire country home.

Amelia, unlike Eliza and Chloe, inherited their father's ability to paint forgeries. When one of her forgeries suddenly became available at a viscount's estate sale, the sisters had been in a panic. But it had attracted the attention of Lord Vale, who had been enamored of Amelia and had hired her to paint his portrait rather than turn her in to the authorities.

The identity of the sisters' criminal father had been revealed to society, but two weddings to wealthy and influential earls had turned what would otherwise be outrageous scandals into romantic fairy tales.

But Chloe's own secrets had remained undisclosed.

Until now.

Not for the first time, she wondered how much the Duke of Cameron knew.

Eliza set the letters aside and looked at Chloe. "Are you certain you are well? You seem anxious."

"Forgive me. I'm just tired."

Eliza brightened. "Perhaps Lady Webster's garden party this afternoon will lift your spirits. She is revealing her new horticultural conservatory, and it should be a sight to see. You haven't forgotten about it, have you? Young Lord Sefton will be in attendance."

"Of course I haven't forgotten." It was another opportunity to flirt with Henry, to try to encourage his pursuit. If all went well, he'd soon officially court her.

Henry fulfilled all her requirements. Many people would disapprove of Chloe's scheming for his title and wealth, but those people would never understand. They'd never known hunger or cold from lack of coal in the brazier. They'd never experienced a prolonged illness or an incessant cough that made their chest feel tight—as if their lungs were being held in someone else's merciless grip.

A thought occurred to Chloe and she twisted her napkin in her lap. "Will the duke accompany Henry?"

Eliza's brow furrowed. "I suppose. I'm told His Grace has taken Henry under his wing. Why?"

Chloe shrugged a shoulder. "Just curious."

"Well, I'm impressed by the young Lord Sefton. Now that Amelia is married, my sole focus will be on finding you a good match," Eliza said.

Eliza had always been earnest about matchmaking for her sisters. She'd been the one to look after them when their father had left. It was Eliza who had devised a new identity as a widow and opened the Peacock Print Shop, an establishment that sold paintings, prints, and bric-a-brac items. If it were not for Eliza's sacrifice they would still be in St. Giles.

Chloe had never minded Eliza's enthusiasm. But Chloe also knew what both Eliza and Amelia whispered about her every time she mentioned an eligible bachelor. *She's searching for a father figure after Father's abandonment.*

Chloe was the youngest, and thus, her memories weren't entirely tarnished by her father's foray into painting forgeries. Vague memories of him reading her bedtime stories lingered in her mind. They'd been close…and perhaps too similar.

The rotten apple doesn't fall far from the ailing tree.

Footsteps sounded outside the hall, and the butler entered the breakfast room for the second time that morning. "There is a delivery for you, Miss Chloe."

Chloe set down her cup. "For me?"

"Yes, miss."

Both sisters pushed back their chairs and followed the butler into the vestibule, where an enormous arrangement of hothouse lilies in a glittering crystal vase rested on a pedestal table.

Chloe gasped. "Oh my! Have you ever seen such lovely blooms?"

"Read the card," Eliza prodded.

Chloe reached for the embossed vellum. For a heart-stopping moment, she wondered if the blooms were sent by the duke.

Don't be ridiculous. There was nothing romantic about

the Duke of Cameron. He had offended and insulted her, and then he had kissed her—not to seduce her or court her, but to prove his dominance and control, to prove that he would win in their battle of wills no matter the tactic chosen. If only she hadn't felt a ripple of desire when he'd pressed his lips to hers.

She broke the seal, let the sheet of crisp paper unfold, and read out loud:

Dear Miss Somerton.

The beauty of these flowers is nothing compared to your own.

Yours truly,
Lord Sefton.

Eliza clasped her hands to her chest in delight. "How utterly romantic! The garden party shall be the perfect opportunity to further encourage the young earl's pursuit."

Chloe's fingers tightened on the card. Her emotions vacillated between satisfaction and uncertainty. Her plans were coming to fruition. And if all went well, Henry would propose marriage before the end of the Season. This was what she wanted, wasn't it?

Then why did she keep remembering a single kiss from an infuriating duke?

Chapter Five

Chloe inhaled the scent of evergreens, azaleas, and flowering shrubs in Lady Webster's garden. She'd arrived with Eliza and Huntingdon a half hour prior and they'd mingled with the dozens of well-dressed guests.

An impressive showing had turned out for the unveiling of Lady Webster's horticultural conservatory, a large glass-and-steel structure that loomed in the distance. A widow in her early fifties, Lady Webster was an avid horticulturist. Dressed entirely in green, she wore a turban that made her look like one of her sculpted evergreens. The conservatory doors remained closed until all had arrived, when Lady Webster would open them for her guests to tour.

It was a lovely mild afternoon with a cloudless sky. Tables in the meticulously kept gardens had been set up with an array of delicacies and refreshments for the guests to enjoy. The women wore colorful gowns of muslin or silk, and the men were dressed in trousers, jackets, and checked and striped waistcoats. Chloe had taken care with her own dress—a yellow muslin with lace at the sleeves, bodice, and hem. Alice had styled her blond curls in an elegant chignon with soft curls brushing her cheeks.

"Do you see Lord Sefton?" Eliza leaned close to whisper in Chloe's ear.

"No." Chloe smoothed her skirts with nervous fingers.

Eliza patted her arm. "Don't fret. He's due to arrive. Would you like me to mention in passing that we plan to ride in Hyde Park tomorrow afternoon? Perhaps he will make an appearance and the two of you can ride together."

For some reason, Eliza's comment did not sit well. "You must not appear to interfere. All is going well on its own."

Eliza blinked. "You're right, of course."

Chloe immediately felt churlish at the flash of hurt in her sister's eyes. "Forgive me, Eliza. I didn't mean to sound ungrateful. I'm simply anxious."

Eliza's brow eased, and she squeezed Chloe's hand. "I promise not to act like an overbearing matchmaking mother."

Scanning the crowd, Chloe searched for Lord Sefton. Her gaze focused on the tallest men present. Henry was average in height, but the duke was tall and muscular and would be easier to find. She didn't see either man.

If Cameron did appear with Henry in tow, would he attempt to bribe her again? Or try another tactic?

Annoyance rose within Chloe. She knew she was too prideful by nature—a bad trait she'd inherited from her father, along with his stubbornness and temper. If the duke wanted a challenge, she would give him a battle.

Huntingdon approached to join Eliza and Chloe. Her brother-in-law was a handsome man, but it was the look of adoration in his eyes when he gazed upon Eliza that had immediately endeared him to Chloe.

"Lord Ruskin is here. He's a generous patron of the Royal Academy, and I need to speak with him," Huntingdon said.

Eliza arched an eyebrow as she looked at a group of

men conversing beside a well-sculpted hedgerow. "I take it he wants your opinion on another piece of artwork he's purchased. Is it his third painting this month?"

"His fourth. I hope he'll loan the Raphael to the museum. Please excuse me."

Chloe had learned that art collectors frequently asked for Huntingdon's opinion. "Good luck," she said as Huntingdon walked away.

Eliza sighed. "I suspect Lord Ruskin will keep my husband occupied for the remainder of the party. I suppose I should speak with Lady Ruskin. Will you come?"

Chloe wrinkled her nose. "As much as I enjoy conversing about art, I think you should go alone. I could use a cool glass of lemonade."

Eliza nodded, and Chloe wandered to a refreshment table where glasses of lemonade awaited for thirsty guests.

"Hello there."

Chloe turned to see a young gentleman with red hair, freckles, and light blue eyes standing behind her. He bowed gallantly. "Lord Fairchild at your service. May I fetch you refreshment, Miss…?"

She recognized him as the eldest of Viscount Fairchild's four sons. Chloe curtsied. "Miss Chloe Somerton."

He had straight teeth and a warm, friendly smile. "It is a pleasure to make your acquaintance."

"Likewise. Lemonade would be lovely," Chloe said.

He reached for a glass and offered it to her. Chloe took a sip and eyed him over the rim of her glass. He was not strikingly handsome, but attractive with touches of humor around his mouth and near his eyes. He was also next in line to the title, and she suspected many debutantes would be clamoring to dance with him at the Season's upcoming balls.

"Are you interested in horticulture?" he asked.

She shook her head. "Goodness, no. I had trouble keeping

alive a potted plant that was a gift for my birthday. Are you?"

He chucked. "I find your honesty refreshing. And no, I attend these events because my mother insists I should."

"That's kind of you to want to please your mother."

"You haven't met the viscountess. I act more out of fear than kindness."

She burst out laughing, then covered her mouth in horror.

He stilled and looked at her. "You have a lovely laugh, Miss Somerton. I have a confession," Fairchild said. "I've been watching you since your arrival."

Her eyes widened. "Oh?" Was he flirting with her?

"To be truthful, other men here have as well."

She sipped her drink. "You flatter me."

"It's the truth."

Her cheeks grew warm. He *was* flirting with her.

The amused look suddenly left Fairchild's eyes, and he took a step closer and touched her arm. "It would be my pleasure to escort you during the conservatory tour."

If all went according to plan, she would be with Henry. "That won't be possible. I promised my sister, Lady Huntingdon," she lied.

"Perhaps I can speak with her and request—" Suddenly Fairchild looked beyond her shoulder, and a crinkle appeared between his brows.

The air seemed altered; it thickened and warmed. She stiffened and slowly turned toward the garden gate, as if she needed to gather her defenses for an anticipated blow. Her gaze connected with the Duke of Cameron's, and despite her resolve to ignore him, her breath hitched. His face was impassive, but his eyes were stormy and fierce as they held hers.

His eyes broke contact with hers to take in Fairchild standing close to her, his hand on her arm. The duke's expression darkened and his jaw hardened. A frisson of fearful anticipation traveled down Chloe's spine. She hadn't realized she'd been holding her breath until the ability to breathe came back in a rush.

For the first time, she noticed Henry standing beside the duke. Henry hadn't yet spotted her and he scanned the crowd, oblivious to the dark look radiating from the man beside him.

Gathering her senses, she set the half-full glass down on the refreshment table and turned to Lord Fairchild. "Excuse me, my lord, but my sister is summoning me." Not waiting for his response, she clutched her skirts and hurried to where Eliza stood conversing with a group of women.

As soon as Eliza spotted Chloe's face, she stepped away. "What is it? Has Lord Sefton arrived?"

She nodded. "Yes. Henry and the duke are here."

"Let's not waste time, then." Eliza smoothed her hair and walked to where both Henry and Cameron stood. Chloe trailed behind, and both men bowed when they spotted the ladies.

Chloe turned to Henry, ignoring, with effort, the duke who seemed to tower above them. "Thank you for the flowers, my lord. They were lovely."

Henry's earnest brown eyes reminded Chloe of an eager puppy wanting to please. "I couldn't decide between flowers or chocolates."

"I do have a sweet tooth," she said.

He pressed a hand to his chest. "A woman after my own heart. May I call on you tomorrow for a ride in the park?"

She smiled. "I'd like that."

Cameron took a step forward and frowned. "You're busy tomorrow."

Henry looked at the duke, baffled. "I don't recall an appointment for tomorrow."

"I'm to show you how to handle the books for your estate, remember? You need to understand your steward's records."

It was clear the duke was not only taking Henry under his wing socially, but also helping him with all matters of his inherited estate after the former earl's demise.

"Did we have that planned? Can't we pick another time?" Henry asked.

"No."

"I understand," Chloe said. "Your estate matters must take precedence."

Distress flashed in Henry's eyes. "Another time—"

"I look forward to it, my lord." She could barely think with the duke standing so close. How on earth could she flirt with Henry with Cameron glaring at her?

For a fearful moment, she wondered if she'd been wrong and he would blurt out her secret to everyone present at the party. He wouldn't dare, would he?

She stole a sidelong glance at Cameron's hard profile. In the unforgiving daylight, the fine lines about his mouth and eyes were visible. It only served to make him more ruggedly handsome. Unbidden memories arose—memories of his firm lips softly caressing hers, of her body pressed against his muscular frame. Why couldn't she forget?

"Lady Webster is opening the conservatory," Eliza said. "Come, we shall all tour it together."

Chloe let out a breath of relief for the distraction. She needed to escape Cameron's razor-like gaze, and she hoped to put distance between them during the tour. Huntingdon approached, and the five of them joined the line of guests waiting to enter the glass-and-steal conservatory. As soon as they stepped inside, humid warmth enveloped them. Sunlight cut a path of light through the glass walls. Long worktables, holding everything from gardening tools, sacks of potting soil, and pots in every size imaginable crowded the center of the space. The scent of flowers, plants, and moist soil hung in the air like heady perfume.

Lady Webster faced her guests as she pointed out different types of plants and flowers and how they flourished within the conservatory. Eliza and Huntingdon ventured closer to the front of the group, and Chloe knew her sister intended to give her time alone with Henry. It would have been a marvelous plan if Cameron had followed suit. But the duke stayed back.

Her eyes were drawn to his broad shoulders in his tailored jacket, and her heartbeat throbbed in her ears. She knew many men padded their jackets to increase the breadth of their shoulders. Heavens, Cameron would never need to instruct his tailor to—

"You look lovely in yellow. It brings out the vibrant gold in your hair."

She dragged her eyes away from Cameron to look at Henry standing beside her. "Thank you." Her voice sounded far away and displaced.

"I promise to find time to visit."

"That would be lovely," she said. "I visit the orphanage on Tuesday and Thursday afternoons only."

"Then I look forward to this Wednesday," Henry said.

"You're forgetting your stables."

A glowering duke turned to face them. Chloe felt her cheeks grow warm. Had he been listening to their conversation?

"Pardon?" Henry asked.

"You need to inspect your horses. Your father purchased several thoroughbreds from Tattersalls. He bred them and had intended to sell the offspring this year."

Henry had a blank look. "Did he?"

"I'd mentioned it before, when we were going over the ledgers, remember?"

By the confused look on Henry's face it was clear he didn't remember or hadn't been paying much attention to the lessons.

"You must finish what your father had started. It requires a trip to your estate in Hertfordshire to deal with the horses," Cameron said.

Distress replaced the look of confusion on Henry's face. "Hertfordshire? When?"

Cameron folded his arms across his chest. "The sooner the better."

Chloe wanted to stomp her foot and curse. She was also tempted to snatch a pot from one of the worktables and smash it over Cameron's head. At this rate, Henry wouldn't be free for the remainder of the Season.

The rest of the tour was an exercise in frustration. Henry remained silent and brooding. Lady Webster droned on and on as she talked about a rare variety of ferns. The temperature of the conservatory continued to climb as the guests grew restless. Chloe attempted to speak with Henry, but with Cameron's constant presence at his elbow, it was nearly impossible.

At last, the tour was over and they left the warm, humid conservatory and stepped outside. A soft breeze blew tendrils of damp hair at her nape and she let out a held-in breath. She wasn't the only one grateful. The sighs of relief from other guests as they exited the glass-and-steel building were audible.

Chloe needed a moment of peace to gather her thoughts. Scanning the lawn, she spotted a garden path. She glanced both ways to ensure no one was watching, then hurried toward the path. It was cool and refreshing beneath a canopy of trees, and she admired the exquisite work of Lady Webster's numerous gardeners. Topiaries, well-trimmed hedgerows, and colorful flowerbeds provided a lovely respite. The sound of running water drew her, and she came upon a pond filled with tiny colorful fish. A white stone bench was situated by the pond, and she sat and smoothed her skirts. Several minutes passed as she watched exotic blue, yellow, and orange fish dart beneath the smooth rocks that lined the bottom of the pond.

Secluded, her thoughts returned to her dilemma. The duke had clearly drawn battle lines and intended to guard Henry. If all went his way, she wouldn't get a moment alone with the young earl. Henry would eventually lose interest and pursue another pretty debutante this Season.

It wasn't going to work. She could outsmart Cameron. It may take questionable tactics, but as he said, there was no room for chivalry or niceties in war.

"So this is where you've been hiding."

She started at the familiar masculine voice and turned to see Cameron step onto the stone path.

Chapter Six

"Why trouble yourself to find me?" Chloe said.

The duke walked forward, all lean muscle and power. "We have unfinished business."

"Do we? I thought everything had been said."

"Not quite."

She stood and faced him squarely. "I came to your home and explained that I am a different person than I was in my youth, but you chose not to believe me. You threatened me to stay away, and when that didn't work, you tried to bribe me."

"And when that didn't work, I kissed you," he said, his voice low and smooth.

She felt an unwelcome surge of excitement. Her memories of the kiss were pure and clear. "I'd rather not talk about that."

"Why? I can't seem to forget about it."

Goodness. She'd felt the same, but she would never admit it.

"Why Henry?" he asked.

Was he serious? Because Henry was young, handsome, kind, titled, and would make a splendid choice for any debutante this Season. Why should *she* be any different?

At her silence, his expression hardened.

"From what I saw, you already have another suitor. Fairchild's heir. You can choose him over Henry."

Was he jealous? The thought should make her turn and flee the gardens like a woman chased by footpads. Instead, it made her skin tighten. "I don't do well with orders."

"That's a shame, because I'm used to having my commands followed."

She raised her chin and eyed him defiantly. "By men. I'm a woman if you haven't noticed."

His gaze raked down her body, then returned to capture her eyes. "Oh, I've noticed."

She flushed as an alarming heat traveled through her limbs. Clearing her throat, she struggled to maintain even ground with him. "That's not what I meant...and you know it, Your Grace."

"Don't call me that. My name is Michael."

Her pulse skittered. "Why on earth would I use your Christian name?" It was entirely improper, scandalously so. But then, nothing about their relationship was proper.

"I'm new to the title. It belongs to my father and brother."

She knew about the tragic carriage accident that had killed his father and brother and left him with a dukedom. Was he devastated to come back unscathed from war only to learn his remaining family wasn't there to welcome him home?

Or maybe he wasn't unscathed. She recalled the strange episode at Bullock's Museum outside the room that housed Napoleon's carriage. He hadn't seemed well...but rather injured in mind, not body. It had struck her as strange behavior for such a dominant and powerful man.

Michael. The name suited him. Not "Your Grace" or "duke" or "Cameron," but simply Michael.

Her gaze dropped to his mouth, and she bit her lower lip.

"You shouldn't do that. It makes me want to kiss you again."

She fought the pull. He was bad for her, and heaven knew, she had been bad enough in her past. She refused to ruin her future. "You are just saying that to distract me, to ruin my chances with Henry."

"I should be, but I mean every word." Reaching out, he trailed a finger down her cheek and then across her bottom lip. She was shocked by the simple touch, gentle and mesmerizing. How could a man with calloused fingers hardened by battle be so gentle?

"I've wanted to touch you all through the conservatory tour," he said. "And here…now…I finally have you alone."

Chloe's eyes widened at his bold words. She opened her mouth to protest, and he dipped his head and pressed his mouth to hers.

Oh God.

He made no move to embrace her. Only his lips touched hers. She was free to step back and end this madness. But she couldn't move, couldn't push him away. The press of his lips was a delicious sensation.

"Do you feel the spark between us?" he murmured huskily. Moving his head back and forth, he brushed her lips with his. Gentle…ever so maddeningly gentle. She fought the urge to lean into the kiss. Her fingers clenched into her fists, her nails digging into her palms rather than running up his arms to grasp his broad shoulders.

"Ah, you do."

Her response was a whimper. This time, when he claimed her mouth, her lips parted on a sigh. He deepened the kiss and pulled her close, wrapping his arms around her waist. The hardness of his chest against her curves was shocking and arousing at once. A frisson of excitement seared through her. Her fists unfurled at his sides and her fingers slid up his arms to delve in his hair. The strands were soft and enticing, in contrast to the hardness of his body. His tongue traced the soft fullness of her lips, warm and sweet.

She sighed. For his cold, battle-hardened appearance, his kisses were as tender and light as a summer breeze. Warm and arousing at once. She should fear him. She should fear for her virtue, her reputation, her very existence in society. But she didn't. Instead, she feared the rapid beat of her pulse at his nearness. The raw hunger in his eyes. The intense physical awareness of each other. The tremor inside her that heated her thighs and groin.

Drugged by his clean and manly scent, she kissed him back, her tongue tangling with his. He groaned and sucked her full bottom lip into his mouth like a ripe berry.

Heavens. She was in over her head, wasn't she?

He lifted his head and looked into her eyes. "I've changed my mind. I won't tell anyone your secret."

She blinked and attempted to slow her rapidly beating heart. He still held her in his arms, and her soft curves were molded to the contours of his lean body.

"You won't?"

"And forget my offer to pay you to leave Henry alone."

"Truly?"

"I want something else from you. What will it take for you to be my lover? Jewels? A Mayfair town house? Name your price."

A tight knot formed within her stomach. She pushed against his chest and took a step back. "You cannot be serious."

"I'm always serious. Do not claim you are innocent. Not after your response to that kiss."

She should slap him. But something about his arrogance sparked her fury. Of course, he thought her sexually experienced. A former thief and daughter of a criminal could never be innocent in his eyes. Why bother to correct him? He'd never believe her. And the kiss had been scintillating... wanton.

Instead, she tried another tactic to dissuade him. "What of Henry? How do you think he'd feel about your proposition?"

His brow creased, and for the first time, she noticed a flash of regret cross his expression. "Do you think I wanted it to be like this? I am supposed to look after Henry, not steal what he believes he wants, but the pull between us is too strong. It may be wrong, illogical even, but I can think of little else."

She met his gaze and saw raw desire in the dark depths of his eyes that made her gasp. Desire that made her feel stripped of her gown, corset, and shift in an instant. Desire that said he couldn't go long without tossing her over his broad shoulder and carrying her off to his bed where he would show her all the secret pleasures to be found in his arms.

For a fleeting instant, she wasn't sure she'd be able to resist him. Then the reality of what he'd offered sank in.

He wanted her to be his *mistress*. He didn't think of her as a lady worthy of marriage. Her traitorous body may shiver at his touch, but she didn't want what he offered. She didn't want to be a kept woman. Mistresses didn't have the security of a man's name or title. They could be abandoned far too easily and left behind with only a few shiny baubles. Her father had already abandoned her, and she would never stand for another man in her life to treat her the same way. She swore never to be a victim to a man's whims again.

But a man as arrogant and sure of himself as the Duke of Cameron—Michael—would never understand. He didn't care if he hurt her or not. He didn't concern himself about her future or what would become of her when she grew old, or heaven forbid, fell ill. She swallowed hard, trying not to reveal her hurt or her anger. She refused to give him the satisfaction. The sudden need to wound him, just as he'd wounded her with his selfish request, welled in her chest.

"You flatter yourself, *Your Grace*. I wouldn't agree to become your lover if you were the last man standing at this party."

"Why?"

"Isn't it obvious? You're far too old, too arrogant, and too jaded for me."

Tossing her head, she fled the gardens.

• • •

Michael stared after Chloe as she fled down the stone path. As soon as he'd arrived at Lady Webster's garden party, he'd searched for her. When he'd spotted her speaking with Lord Fairchild, a cold knot had formed in his gut. The man had been too damned close, and his hand had rested possessively on Chloe's arm. Michael's instinctive reaction had been strong.

Jealousy.

The foreign emotion was as unsettling as it was uncomfortable. He was never possessive over a woman. No one had ever intrigued him enough to care. But Chloe Somerton was magnificent, unlike every other young lady at this ridiculous party. A large part of him admired her grit. The rest of him fiercely desired her.

He'd been right. She was not a virginal miss, and she hadn't protested when he claimed she wasn't innocent. Her past was too unsavory, and she was lucky she'd escaped the hangman's noose. Rather than dissuade him, it only made her infinitely more interesting. He'd found himself hovering nearby in the conservatory tour, interrupting Henry's attempts to court her.

He was still surprised at his own offer to make her his mistress. The thought had churned in his mind, but he hadn't intended to voice it until he'd seen her with Fairchild. Now that the offer had been made, he knew it was the perfect solution.

He refused to marry with his condition. The fits were increasing in frequency. But he needn't worry about a mistress. He'd only see her when he was certain an episode would not occur, and unlike a wife, he could leave at any time. Meanwhile, their shared attraction was strong and mutual. No one would know of their secret liaison.

Michael's only hesitation was Henry. The young man had his heart set on Chloe, and Michael struggled with remorse. He tried to push his guilt aside. Henry didn't know about her colorful past or that she was using him for his newfound title and wealth. He believed her innocent, and she acted the part to perfection.

Whatever doubts Michael had that she would make a good match for Henry multiplied after their second heated kiss. Chloe Somerton needed a man who could match her mettle. Not a fawning admirer who would send flowers and read poetry and bend to her every demand. She'd quickly tire of such a companion. No, she needed a man who could tame her wild rebelliousness while unleashing her hidden passion.

Too old, be damned.

She'd challenged him. Again. He wondered what it would take for her to accept.

Chapter Seven

Deep in the recesses of her subconscious, Chloe knew she was dreaming.

She stood in an alley between a haberdashery and milliner's and watched as pedestrians rushed from one shop to another on the busy street to escape the cold. She had gotten bolder over time. The handkerchief had been worth a few shillings, a pair of kidskin leather gloves a bit more, and a gold button the most. But now she needed to set her sights on something bigger.

She would have ceased taking greater risks, but the tonic she needed was almost finished, and Eliza would have to purchase more for her from Mr. Allenson at the apothecary.

A gust of wind blew through the streets and down the alley. Wisps of hair flew into her face. Shivering, she clasped her thin cloak tighter to her chest. She'd have to hurry before Eliza and Amelia noticed her missing from the print shop. The winter hadn't been kind to their business. The merchants and middle class who visited the Peacock Print Shop for paintings, prints, and bric-a-brac items for their homes rarely ventured out in this weather. With little income, the three sisters had had to ration food and coal for the brazier. Their living quarters, upstairs from the print shop, had an ever-present chill.

Chloe coughed. Once she started, it was difficult to stop. The cough racked her lungs, made her chest squeeze painfully until the simple act of breathing took concentration and effort. It took five minutes for the cough to subside and her lungs to ease. She pulled a glass bottle from her skirt pocket and uncorked it. The distasteful smell of the apothecary's tonic made her wrinkle her nose. The bottle was light, only a few drops of the tonic remained, and Chloe drank the precious drops. If she were lucky, the medicine would work for a few hours. She slipped the empty bottle into her skirt pocket.

A fine, crested carriage stopped in front of the haberdashery. A pair of well-matched bays snorted in the cold air and steam rose from their nostrils. The driver hopped down to open the door and lowered the step. Two women stepped out, a mother and daughter. They pulled the hoods of their fur-lined cloaks over their heads as they hurried into the shop and out of the cold.

Just in time.

Chloe followed the pair into the shop. The shopkeeper, a thin man with bushy eyebrows and a square forehead, approached to help the women. From the fine quality of their clothing, she suspected they were nobility. Perhaps the wife and daughter of a marquess, an earl…or a duke.

Chloe smiled and made eye contact with the shopkeeper, then feigned interest in a simple straw bonnet with blue ribbon on one of the tall shelves.

"No, Mother. That hat is hideous and makes my complexion look pallid," the girl whined.

The hat in question was puke green with a bright orange ribbon. Chloe agreed with the daughter. The hat was quite ugly and *did* make the blonde look ashen.

"Nonsense," the mother snapped. "It's perfect for a ride in Hyde Park during the promenade hour. Try it on, my dear."

The daughter pouted.

"You do want to attract Lord Barker, don't you?"

"Fine," the girl snapped. She removed her bonnet and attempted to try on the hat, but she had trouble. "It's catching on my pin."

Chloe's eyes were instantly drawn to a jeweled pin in the daughter's hair. The opal stone glowed iridescent in the afternoon light from the bay window.

The girl removed the pin from her hair and dropped it on a table among a collection of ribbons as if it were worthless.

Perfect. Chloe stared at the jeweled pin longingly then watched the shopkeeper out of the corner of her eye. He licked his lips, clearly eager to satisfy his wealthy customers and make a sale.

Chloe's hand slipped into her skirt pocket and touched the smooth glass bottle. She knew Eliza and Amelia would willingly give up a meal to pay for more medicine. But how could Chloe allow them to go hungry?

She couldn't. Wouldn't. Not when taking something so small from someone so wealthy could aid them all.

Waiting until the shopkeeper was occupied with the demanding daughter and her desperate mother, Chloe made her move. She walked to the table, picked up a pink ribbon lying next to the pin, and ran it through her fingers as if considering buying it. The daughter spotted other hats, and she began to argue with her mother about the color of the artificial flowers she preferred.

What would it be like to worry about bonnets and ornamentation rather than where they were going to get the next month's rent?

Chloe's hand hovered over the opal pin. A strand of curly fair hair was entwined with it. Her heart thundered in her chest as her fingers grasped the pin and slipped it into her skirt pocket.

She headed straight for the door and, reaching up, held the little bell so that it wouldn't jingle as she slipped outside. She made it into the alley before she let out a breath.

Success!

It had started raining, but she decided not to head back to the print shop just yet. The apothecary was only two doors down. But Mr. Allenson wouldn't want an opal pin. She kept walking until she ended up in front of a plain brick building that housed one of the renowned houses of ill repute in the city—the Seven Sins brothel. Only one person would give her the money in exchange for the stolen pin. The proprietress, Madame Satine, was always willing to—

"Stop! Thief!"

Sheer black fright swept through her. Heart pounding, she began sprinting through the streets. She dared a glimpse over her shoulder to spot a constable in full pursuit. Rain gathered in between the cobblestones, turning them slick and treacherous. A cat darted across her path, and she slipped and fell to one knee. She cried out in pain as her thin stocking tore and she cut her knee, but then she sprang up and continued running. If she were caught, she would be dragged before a magistrate and sent to Newgate. Her sisters would be beside themselves.

Footsteps sounded closer. A man's heavy breathing.

She looked again. And cried out in terror.

The Duke of Cameron was behind her.

"Got you!" he cried out, as he grasped her shoulder and whirled her to face him. His muscular frame towered above her, his face fierce, and satisfaction flashed in his black eyes. "Now you are mine. Body and soul."

His black eyes licked over her like a candle flame. Her fear vanished beneath his heated gaze and her skin grew hot.

She tossed a damp curl across her shoulder and met his stare. "Never!"

"Challenge accepted. I warn you that I intend to make love to you."

His dark, compelling looks took her breath away. The tip of her tongue traced her lips in a provocative gesture. A thrill of satisfaction coursed through her when his pupils dilated and his fingers tightened on her shoulder. "It will be an epic battle," she challenged.

"It's good, then, that I'm a fierce fighter."

He pulled her into his arms and captured her mouth with demanding mastery. Her lips clung to his and opened softly under the seductive pressure of his passionate kiss. His hands greedily explored her waist, her hips. She moaned, pressing her soft curves against the hard planes of his magnificent body.

He lifted his head to look into her eyes. "I hereby seize the prize."

Chloe woke in a sweat. Her breathing was ragged and her heart thundered in her chest. What had started as a nightmare of being chased through the streets by a constable with a stolen pin in her pocket had turned into an erotic experience. She couldn't believe how real it had seemed. Even now she could feel the strength of his arms, taste his kiss. She already thought of the duke more often than she'd like when she was awake.

Now, he'd invaded her dreams.

Chapter Eight

The hackney stopped before a red brick building with black shutters. Chloe peered out the window. A black sign with white letters read: WHITLESON'S HOME FOR ORPHANED GIRLS. The orphanage was located in a part of the city that had once been affluent but now was run-down. In the distance a church bell tolled. Ever-present smoke from the London factories marred the sky. Stepping from the hackney, she made her way up the front steps and entered the building.

A heavyset woman with brown curls fading to gray came forward to greet Chloe. Mrs. Porter was one of the teachers and caretakers of the younger girls at the orphanage. "It's good to see you back, Miss Somerton. I'm sure Emily will be pleased."

"Emily is a sweet child. I've grown attached to her in my last few visits. How is her health?" Chloe asked.

A shadow crossed Mrs. Porter's face. "Not well, I'm afraid. She remains listless and has little appetite. No one can explain the lethargy or the weakness in her limbs."

Chloe's chest tightened. "What does the physician say?"

"Dr. Evans visits every Wednesday, miss. He believes Emily is of a weak disposition and he warned that she may never grow to be as strong or healthy as the other girls."

Chloe couldn't accept such a diagnosis. Emily was too young, too lovely a child. "Perhaps another physician, then—"

Mrs. Porter wrung her hands. "I must wait until Mr. Whitleson returns. Now that his wife has passed away, he makes all the decisions regarding the staff and the finances for the orphanage."

Chloe had never met Mr. Whitleson. Since her return to town from Huntingdon's country estate, he'd been away. His wife had founded the orphanage. He took over afterward, but relied on Mrs. Porter and the other staff to provide the day-to-day care of the children. Still, he controlled the finances of the orphanage, and as such, she needed to speak with him regarding the services of the orphanage doctor.

"When will Mr. Whitleson return?" Chloe asked.

"He is visiting a friend in Kent but is expected back in a week's time. I shall speak with him regarding Emily as soon as he returns."

"Thank you." Chloe headed down the corridor. She passed workers and servants and young girls. The orphanage was home to girls, from infants up to seventeen years old. Chloe knew most were never adopted and grew up to work in the orphanage or to toil long hours in the factories.

A girl of about fifteen, who was carrying a bucket of water and a mop, smiled shyly at Chloe as she hurried past. No doubt she was on her way to her morning chores.

Chloe watched the girl disappear around the corner. She had been close to the child's age when Jonathan Miller had abandoned his three daughters and fled London rather than face arrest for his crimes of forgery. If not for Eliza and Amelia, would Chloe have ended up in an orphanage just like this one?

Gooseflesh rose on her arms that had nothing to do with the cold, damp corridor. She kept on, her steps quicker, until she reached the wing for the younger girls and entered a room. Rows of simple wooden beds with straw mattresses lined both sides of the long room. Each bed was empty and tidily made with white linens and a coarse brown blanket.

Save one.

A small child lay sleeping in the last bed.

The other girls were occupied with their daily chores, then their exercises for the day. But nine-year-old Emily Higgins remained behind to linger abed. It was horribly unfair.

But then, life wasn't fair, was it?

It was a bitter lesson Chloe had learned years ago.

Chloe approached Emily's bedside and watched the sleeping girl. Dark curls contrasted with her pale skin. Her eyelids were as fragile as paper, and long eyelashes formed crescents against her skin. Her small chest rose and fell, her breathing labored. Even ill, she was a beautiful child, and Chloe felt a tug in the center of her chest.

Reaching out, she touched the girl's small hand. "Hello, Emily."

Eyelashes fluttered open to reveal jewel-green eyes. A second passed, then pink lips formed a perfect O. "Miss Chloe! I'm so happy you're here."

Emily struggled to sit up and raised her arms. Chloe's heart tugged as she embraced the girl's small frame. The strong scent of rhubarb ointment that the nurse had rubbed on Emily's chest wafted to Chloe.

"How do you feel?" Chloe asked.

Emily coughed. "The nurse says I'm not well enough to join the other girls. I don't like staying in bed."

A knot formed in Chloe's throat. "I'm sorry, sweetheart." Everyone at the orphanage believed that Emily was born sickly. Chloe refused to believe it. There had to be a medical explanation for the child's lethargy and weak lungs. Every time Emily attempted to join the other girls outside, she would start wheezing and gasping for breath. Then the coughing fits would start and she would lack the energy to do anything more than walk.

Chloe pulled up a wooden chair and sat at Emily's bedside. "I made some pictures for you." Chloe pulled out small lithographs of a young girl Emily's age playing with a hoop. The skill with a burin was a talent she had learned from her father. She wasn't a gifted artist like her sister, Amelia, but she enjoyed creating artwork as a pastime.

"It's beautiful. Is it really for me?"

"Yes. You can look at it anytime. I hope it lifts your spirits."

"What else do you have?"

"I brought a book of fairy tales. Would you like me to read to you?"

"Oh yes. My mother used to read to me before she got sick and went to Heaven. Do you remember your mother?"

Chloe rested the book on her lap. "I have vague memories. She was kind and loving and gave lots of hugs. But she passed when I was young."

"What about your father?" Emily asked.

Chloe's fingers tightened around the book's spine. "My father was an artist. I remember when he taught me how to draw and use a burin to engrave a picture. He knew I preferred engraving to charcoal sketching, but the truth was I did it to please him. It was never my strongest interest. I would much rather have climbed a tree in our garden or fed the horses carrots in the mews."

Emily smiled. "That sounds like fun. How old were you when he died?"

"He never died. At least not that I've heard. He left us."

"Oh," Emily said. "I never knew my father, either."

"Then we have that in common as well."

"What else do we have in common, Miss Chloe?

Chloe hesitated, debating how much to tell. "I was sickly as a child."

"You were?"

If her story could give Emily hope, then she should share it with her. "It started as a simple cold, but I soon developed a cough. Then the cough lingered and lingered and wouldn't go away. A doctor said I had weak lungs. But now I'm healthy."

Emily's lower lip trembled. "I don't know if I'll ever be healthy, Miss Chloe."

"Never say that." Chloe's voice was firm. She refused to believe the child would suffer forever, or worse, die. As she gazed down at Emily, her throat ached. She clutched Emily's hand. "Please promise that you will never give up hope."

"I promise." Emily's little fingers entwined with hers, and the motion felt like a squeeze to Chloe's heart.

"Shall I read?" Chloe asked.

Emily nodded and leaned against her pillow.

Chloe picked up the book and opened it to the first chapter. She swallowed the lump in her throat and smiled. "Once upon a time, in a kingdom far, far away, there lived a beautiful princess…"

• • •

Later that afternoon, Chloe returned to her sister's home in Mayfair. The butler came forward to take her cloak. Sunlight glinted off the magnificent crystal chandelier and cast a kaleidoscope of color on the marble floor. The contrast between the scratched wood floorboards of the orphanage and the black-and-white marble of Huntingdon's vestibule never ceased to amaze her. Her memories of her lodgings in the rookeries of St. Giles lingered in the back of her mind like specters in a closet that could never entirely be forgotten.

"There's a package for you, Miss Chloe," the butler said. "I put it in the drawing room."

"Thank you, Mr. Burke."

Another package? Her curiosity rose as she entered the drawing room to find a box wrapped in lovely flowered paper. The simple card was embossed vellum, and she broke the seal.

My dearest Chloe,

Indulge your fancy for sweets.

Yours fondly,
Henry

He'd used her Christian name and signed it with his own. Surely it was a good sign. She picked up the package and tore the paper to discover a box of chocolates from a popular confectioner. She reached for a piece of dark chocolate, her favorite.

"Your admirer is quite romantic."

Chloe turned to see Eliza in the doorway. "It's from Lord Sefton."

Eliza smiled. "First flowers, now chocolates. If we are fortunate, badly written poetry will come next."

Chloe looked at the treat in her hand nestled in delicate paper. She loved chocolate as much as the next woman, but for some reason she had no desire to taste the sweet.

"What's wrong?" Eliza asked.

Chloe returned the chocolate to the box. "I visited the orphanage today."

"Is it the young girl? Emily is her name?"

Chloe sighed. "Yes. She's still ill, and they are not certain if she will ever be as healthy as the other girls."

Eliza came close and touched her sleeve. "I'm sorry, Chloe. I know how much the child means to you."

Chloe experienced a nauseating sinking of despair, and she closed the box. "I think I'll save these for her. Maybe they will increase her appetite."

"That's very thoughtful. If there is anything Emily needs, please ask. Clothing, shoes, funds for the doctor."

"Thank you. But she rarely leaves her bed, and one pair of shoes is sufficient. She has enough clothing as well, and the orphanage doctor visits weekly."

"Do not lose hope. You were ill as a child, remember?"

How could she forget? It had been devastating, not just the illness but the consequences for her sisters. Eliza and Amelia had never complained, but they'd gone to bed cold and hungry too often because they'd sacrificed for her.

Chloe swallowed. "Yes, I won't give up hope." She turned to Eliza. "Now what is it you came to tell me? Or were you simply curious about the package?"

"I have good news that I hope will cheer you. We are visiting Vauxhall Gardens tonight to see the sensational Madame Saqui."

"The French tightrope dancer?" Chloe's interest was immediately piqued. She'd heard stories about the famous acrobat who achieved enormous acclaim at Covent Garden Theatre when she'd walked from the stage to the top gallery on a tightrope. It would be Chloe's first visit to Vauxhall Gardens, and the knowledge that she would see Madame Saqui perform lifted her spirits.

Eliza clasped her hands. "There's more. Huntingdon invited Lord Sefton to join us."

Henry would be there. Chloe could thank him for the chocolates. Perhaps dance with him in front of the pavilion. But just as quickly as the thought entered her mind, another followed. If Henry came along, then there was a good chance that—

"The duke will be accompanying him as well," Eliza said.

Unbidden images of Chloe's erotic dream rushed back. Michael's calloused fingers as he grasped her shoulders. The raw hunger in his dark eyes as he looked at her. His mouth claiming hers as she moaned her pleasure and need.

"I know what you're thinking," Eliza said.

Chloe's eyes snapped to her sister and she felt her face flush. "You do?"

"Yes. You're concerned that if the Duke of Cameron attends, then you won't have a moment alone with young Henry. I didn't miss what happened at Lady Webster's party."

"You didn't?" Heavens, did her sister witness Chloe's kiss in the gardens with the duke?

"You didn't have a moment alone in the horticultural conservatory. The imposing duke shadowed you and Henry for the entire tour."

Relief coursed through Chloe. *Thank goodness that's all she saw.*

As for tonight, Chloe *should* have been concerned that Michael would prevent her from sneaking off into Vauxhall Gardens alone with Henry, but that wasn't what she was thinking at all. She was too occupied with thoughts of Michael's kiss…how their tongues rolled together, soft and slow…

The trouble was Henry was far from her thoughts. But Michael—she was beginning to think of him more and more by that name—had offered her a position as his mistress.

His mistress!

The offer was as humiliating as it was offending. Never had she both despised and desired someone as she did him.

It was maddening.

She'd never be duchess material to him. Any wife he took would have bloodlines traced back to King Henry VIII.

"You needn't worry," Eliza said, once again interrupting her thoughts. "I've invited a young widow, Lady Willowby, to join us. I have it on good account that she has set her sights on the duke, and I'm confident she'll occupy him so that you will be free to spend time with Lord Sefton."

Chloe masked her inner turmoil with a deceptive calm. She should be grateful for her sister's aid. Then why did she feel as if all the eager anticipation of her first visit to Vauxhall Gardens had vanished?

Eliza smiled. "So you see? It will be a perfect evening."

Chloe swallowed. "Yes, of course." Reaching down, she gathered her resolve. Eliza was right. This was what she wanted—an evening to further cultivate Henry's interest. She would get to walk alone with him in the sculpted gardens by moonlight and lamplight and get to know him better. She realized she knew very little about Henry. She didn't know his ambitions or plans for the future. Here was her chance to spend time together. Perhaps even share a stolen kiss and erase the touch of another.

Michael was confusing her, making her desire what she shouldn't. It was all a lie. A cruel, vicious lie to get her to avoid Henry and abandon her hopes and dreams. The duke cared nothing for her, other than to satisfy his base needs. He wanted her to fail and was doing his best to seduce her to ruin.

She'd best not forget it.

Chapter Nine

That evening, Chloe, Eliza, and Huntingdon took a boat ride across the Thames. A boatman, a war veteran with a wooden leg, rowed the small craft quickly across the river. Soon they passed through the water entrance of Vauxhall Gardens and arrived at the quayside. Lord Huntingdon jumped out and assisted the two women to dry land.

Chloe smoothed the skirts of her gown, a sapphire silk trimmed in Brussels lace that shimmered beneath the moonlight. Her fair hair was fashioned in loose curls and held back by jeweled clips that had been a gift from her sister Amelia on her birthday.

"The duke, Lord Sefton, and Lady Willowby will join us in my private supper box," Huntingdon said.

Chloe had since learned that Lady Willowby was only two years older than she. The youngest of four unmarried daughters of a wealthy merchant, her status had been significantly elevated upon her marriage to a much older viscount. The death of her husband, six months later, had left Lady Willowby a handsome widow's portion and a wealthy lady.

Chloe trailed behind her sister and brother-in-law as they walked to the entrance to the gardens, and Huntingdon paid the fee to enter. She should be grateful if Eliza's manipulations were successful. Lady Willowby would occupy Michael, and Chloe could finally spend time with Henry.

She had little time to ponder the feelings of unease in her stomach as they passed through the entranceway, and she halted at the sight before her.

Hundreds of lanterns hung from trees, masts, and wooden poles to illuminate acres of meticulously landscaped gardens. The magnificent shining lights looked like twinkling stars in the distance. Sycamore, lime, and elm trees lined gravel paths and invited leisurely walks by visitors. Scattered among the trees were wooden arbors that provided shade from the sun in the day and a private spot for an amorous couple in the evening. In the distance, a Roman-styled piazza was lit by dozens of lanterns. Notably absent was the ever-present noise, the unpleasant stench of the city, and the black coal factory smoke that polluted the London air.

They walked farther into the gardens and came to a large open space with a tall multistoried rotunda. An orchestra played in a balcony while well-dressed guests and revelers danced a country reel below. Facing the orchestra, row after row of supper boxes, which could easily hold eight people, were decorated with exquisite paintings from accomplished artists William Hogarth and Francis Hayman. Visitors drank, ate, and strolled through the gardens.

Chloe's eyes were wide as she took in the scene for the first time—all her senses heightened to the sound of the music, the glow of the lanterns, and the scent of flowering shrubs and greenery of the famous pleasure gardens.

Eliza led Chloe toward one of the supper boxes. "I see them," Eliza said.

Chloe turned to see both Henry and Michael approach through the crowd. Henry looked dashing in a bottle-green jacket and striped waistcoat. His fair hair was combed in the *à la Brutus* style currently popular with the dandies of the *ton*.

Guests parted, and the duke came fully into view. Chloe sucked in a breath.

His muscular six-foot frame was complemented by a blue jacket of kerseymere, a striped waistcoat, and trousers that hugged his strong legs. His dark hair shone like mahogany beneath the lamplight, and his sensual dark eyes appeared mysterious and fathomless. He was all lean muscle, power, and confidence. Standing next to him, Henry looked like a boy.

Henry bowed and lifted Chloe's gloved hand to brush a kiss across the satin. "You look lovely as always."

Chloe's lips curled in a welcoming smile. "The chocolates were delectable."

Henry leaned close to whisper. "I hope to learn all your favorites."

She experienced a heightened awareness of Michael as he stepped forward. No doubt he didn't approve of Henry whispering anything into her ear. She turned to properly greet the infuriating duke.

Chloe swallowed. His rapier gaze raked her form-fitting sapphire gown, then captured her eyes. The only sign of his reaction was the slight flaring of his nostrils. "Miss Somerton."

Electric tingles rushed through her at his look. He must have sensed it, for one dark eyebrow arched upward.

She became aware of a rustle of skirts and a lady watching them. "Thank you for inviting me this evening," Lady Willowby said, gliding forward.

She was a beautiful woman with upswept red hair and green eyes. Unlike many with such flame-colored hair, Lady Willowby's fair complexion was like fine china. Not a freckle marred her porcelain skin. Her voluptuous figure was on display in a green gown with a scandalously low bodice that matched the shade of her jade eyes. She looked up at the duke with a mixture of lust and possession.

Chloe hated her instantly.

A waiter approached with a tray of drinks. Eliza was first to pluck a glass from the tray and waited until everyone was served. "We shall order first, then walk the gardens before Madame Saqui's performance. But first let us share a drink of Vauxhall's famous arrack punch." She raised her glass. "To good friends."

Chloe sipped her drink composed of rum, lemon, sugar, and arrack. It was potent, but delicious, and warmed her blood and eased her nerves.

Lady Willowby placed a hand on Michael's sleeve. "Will you escort me through the gardens, Your Grace?"

Michael's expression was unreadable. The only indication he gave that he heard the beautiful widow was a slight nod of his head.

Henry offered Chloe his arm. "Shall we?"

She placed her gloved fingers on his arm, and the three couples headed for the winding gravel paths. Lamps lit the way, and the scent of fruit bushes and perfumed flowers filled the air. It was the perfect setting for adventure, intrigue, and romance.

An odd twinge of disappointment tightened Chloe's chest. She should be pleased. There would be opportunity to be isolated in one of the shadowed paths away from the crowd. But that meant Lady Willowby was free to do the same with Michael.

She frowned. What was wrong with her? After two kisses, she couldn't allow him to ruin her chances of a successful marriage match. He wanted a mistress.

Not a wife.

"I have many fond memories of the pleasure gardens," Henry said. "My father used to bring me here as a boy. Of course, we visited in the daytime back then." A look of sadness crossed his face in the lamplight.

"I'm sorry for your loss. You must miss him," Chloe said.

"I do. He was a good father."

Chloe's fingers tensed. Her father *had* been good. It was only after her mother died—when Chloe was five—that he'd begun to forge priceless works of art. He'd changed then, had become greedy and hadn't cared about whom he harmed with his schemes—clients or his own children.

Henry must have sensed her discomfort. He took her hand in his. "I'm sorry. I didn't mean to bring up unwanted memories. I want you to know that your father's past does not matter to me."

Not for the first time, she recognized that he was kind and considerate, and a marriage with the Earl of Sefton would be amicable and pleasant.

A trill of laughter up ahead drew her interest. Lady Willowby was clinging to the duke's arm. She licked her painted lips and leaned forward, her breasts threatening to spill from her low-cut bodice.

Chloe's blood pounded and heat rose in her face. Henry spoke, but Chloe had difficulty following the conversation. Her eyes kept returning to Michael and the clinging widow. As she watched, Lady Willowby tugged Michael's arm and urged him to turn down a winding path out of view. Chloe's step faltered.

Henry noticed their departure from the main path. Huntingdon and Eliza were paces ahead, oblivious to the departure of the third couple.

"Shall we do the same? I see a path to explore," Henry whispered, and ushered her in a different direction. She followed, determined to stop thinking of the other couple.

Fewer lanterns lit the back paths, and it was darker here. Henry halted beneath a wooden boat that was artfully hung above a branch of an oak tree to pass as an arbor. Tall hedges offered privacy. "I'd like to kiss you, Chloe. May I?"

This was it. A true test. She'd only kissed one man. Would Henry's lips make her feel dizzy with desire? Would her heart pound, her knees weaken, and her breasts tingle?

Closing her eyes, she raised her mouth to his. The pressure of his lips was light and pleasant. She pressed a hand against his slender chest and felt his heart beat fast beneath his waistcoat. At her touch, he moaned and pulled her closer, and the kiss changed. Sloppy, wet kisses slanted over her mouth and down her throat, leaving a slick path on her skin. She fought the urge to push him away. She felt no spark. No rush of wicked, forbidden longing. His chest wasn't hard and solid, like another's, and the touch didn't make her skin sizzle.

A swooping dread settled in her stomach. There was no comparison with Michael's seductive kisses that had left her burning with desire and with an aching need for more.

A rustle of skirts sounded close by. They jumped apart just as the duke and Lady Willowby turned the corner and stopped short. Michael's gaze traveled over Chloe and Henry, and her cheeks grew hot beneath his knowing stare. Chloe's nervousness grew.

Did he know Henry had led her to the isolated path for a stolen kiss?

Michael glowered, his expression fierce. Lady Willowby appeared out of breath and confused, as if she'd been dragged along the gravel path.

"Time to go," Michael said, his voice harsh. "The tightrope dancer is about to begin her performance."

Chloe met Michael's gaze. A scowl pulled at the corners of his lips...lips that could make her long for dangerous things that a lady should never even think of. Lips that made her feel so much more than Henry's kisses.

Oh God. Why him? Why the man who wanted her, but only as his mistress? The man who thought her a lying thief who would forever be beneath him? How could this have happened?

The two couples returned to the rotunda and joined Huntingdon and Eliza. A throng of visitors had gathered in the open space. Chloe's thoughts were of her dilemma and she was slow to comprehend the hushed whispers of the crowed or to notice that all eyes were trained high above.

"Do you see the rope?" Henry pointed to a mast set up at the eastern end of the gardens to another mast half way down one of the main walks.

Chloe looked up. "I do."

"Don't look away. She will show shortly."

Suddenly Madame Saqui appeared on the rope and gave a jaunty wave. A tiny woman with dark hair, her costume was brilliantly spangled and her headdress of colorful feathers reached a considerable height. The orchestra began playing a lively tune, and the crowed burst into cheer. Chloe watched, amazed, as the French ropedancer ran down the inclined rope with grace and an astonishing sense of balance. She twirled and lifted a leg, and the crowd's gasps of delight echoed throughout the night. Chloe was riveted to the sight and was stunned by the Frenchwoman's athleticism.

The act continued for twenty more minutes. Chloe turned to seek out Eliza when she spotted Lady Willowby beside Michael instead. The widow touched his arm, batted her lashes at him, and whispered in his ear.

Chloe's stomach tightened with an emotion she refused to acknowledge. She whirled back around. Determined to ignore them and put distance between them, she took several steps away.

The crowed thickened as more and more people pressed

closer to get a better look at Madame Saqui's act. A burly man with a beaver hat bumped into her and she was separated from Henry.

"What's a pretty one like you doing in the gardens alone tonight?" A pox-faced man asked. He was dressed well, probably gentry, but the strong odor of alcohol wafted from him.

"I'm not alone, sir."

"You have a protector, then? I shall outbid him," he said with great bravado. He tried to take her hand, but Chloe slipped away. During their ownership of the Peacock Print Shop, men had tried to proposition each of the three unmarried proprietors. Chloe had experience with over-amorous customers. But the crush of people tonight unnerved her, and she frantically scanned the crowd to find Henry, Eliza, or Huntingdon.

Just as fear began to take hold, a strong hand grasped her arm. She whirled to find Michael towering over her.

"This way."

She had no trouble following him. Even in a crowd, his presence was compelling. Men and women parted at his size and the air of command that exuded from his tall frame. She assumed he would take her back to the supper box, but he led her away from the throng of people and down a gravel pathway into the gardens.

Her step faltered. "Where are we going?"

"We need to talk. Alone."

Chapter Ten

Panic welled in Chloe's chest. "I don't want to be alone with you." She couldn't trust herself near Michael. The pull of attraction was too strong. Then there was the issue of Lady Willowby. He'd gone off in one of the private hedges with her alone. Did he think he could be with the voluptuous widow and then attempt to seduce Chloe as well?

He abruptly stopped to face her, and she nearly collided with his powerful body. "Did you kiss Henry?"

She bristled at his tone as much as his question. "That's none of your concern."

"Did you kiss him, dammit?" His tone was harsh, his expression like granite. A muscle ticked at his jaw.

"Did you kiss Lady Willowby?"

"Why? Are you jealous?"

"Do not flatter yourself, Your Grace." She pushed away from him, widening the space between them.

"How long will you convince yourself that we aren't meant to be together?" The hoarseness of his tone was like a hot caress across her skin.

"Your arrogance is astounding." She spun around, intending to flee, but her slipper caught on a rock and she stumbled. He latched onto her wrist to steady her, and the simple touch nearly buckled her knees.

"It may be wrong, but I'm honest enough to acknowledge the attraction between us. Are you brave enough to acknowledge it as well, to admit the truth?" At her silence, satisfaction glinted in his coal eyes. "I've never forced a woman into my bed, and I won't start now. Will you be my lover, Chloe?"

A tremor inside her heated her thighs and groin at his erotic offer. She wanted to yield to the burning sweetness that seemed captive within her. She fought it.

"It's not possible." Her voice sounded weak to her own ears.

"Why? You do not strike me as the type of woman who prefers flattery and false praise. You would tire of any man who spews poetry and writes sonnets about the shade of your lips or the blueness of your eyes."

"You misunderstand. What I want is to be more than a man's mistress."

"I'll give you everything."

Everything but a wedding ring.

I refuse to spend a future worrying about money or security or if he'll leave, she vowed. *I'll never allow myself to become a victim of a man's abandonment again!*

What she felt for Michael was desire. Lust. Nothing more could come of it. Certainly not a future. If she gave her innocence to him, she would lose the most valuable thing she possessed for her future husband. And after Michael tired of her, she'd be left behind with a few trinkets and a ruined reputation.

The man saw her only as a pickpocket. A thief. Someone out for Henry's title and fortune. A woman who'd been with other men.

Regret seared her chest. No matter how hard she tried, she'd never be good enough, would she?

"You want a ring?" he asked.

"Is that so hard to imagine?"

He shook his head. "I cannot have a wife."

Something about his tone made the hair on her nape stand on end. He couldn't have a wife or didn't want a wife? The difference was subtle, but there nonetheless.

"What—"

"We do not need to marry to share pleasure. It will be our secret. No one will learn of it. Let me show you how good it can be between us."

He stepped close and her traitorous heart skipped a beat. The strength and power of his will was as undeniable as the man himself. The glow from the lanterns highlighted his high cheekbones and the perfection of his lips. His gaze was intense and focused on her. Heat emanated from his body, and her skin tingled with awareness. The rakish fall of dark hair across his brow made her want to touch it. Despite her resolve to show no weakness and resist the pull between them, her breaths came short and fast.

His head lowered inch by inch until he hovered above her mouth. "I'm going to kiss you, Chloe Somerton."

Yes. Oh yes.

The night was shattered with a loud *boom.*

Michael's head snapped up. "What the hell—"

She glanced up to see a burst of color light the sky. Madame Saqui and her feathered headdress were illuminated in a spectacular sparkling shower of colorful light. Chloe's heart leaped in her chest. "Fireworks!"

She turned back to Michael. He stood still, his expression frozen, dazed. His eyes were open, and he was looking at her, not the fireworks, but he didn't appear to see a thing. A wheezing sound reverberated from his chest, and perspiration beaded on his brow. Something was wrong, very wrong.

"Your Grace?"

No response.

"Michael?"

Nothing. He was having some kind of episode. The skin around his eyes and mouth pulled tight, and his chest rose and fell with labored breaths. He looked fierce and more than a bit frightening, and for a pulse-pounding moment she could envision him on the battlefield just before he charged the enemy.

Her mind turned back to the time at Bullock's Museum when she'd stepped out of the room housing Napoleon's gilded carriage. He had the same look of panic and fierceness—the pupils dilated and perspiration collected on his brow as if he were reliving an awful memory or nightmare.

She knew all about bad memories that a person couldn't shake and nightmares that made one dread going to bed and blowing out the candle to face the darkness on one's own. A heaviness centered in her chest at his distress.

What was wrong with him? The urge—the desperate need—to somehow aid him and ease his torment was undeniable. Reaching up, she placed her hands on his broad shoulders and did the only thing that came to mind—she kissed him.

His lips were warm and soft beneath hers, but his breathing was still labored. She cradled his face in her hands and increased the pressure of her kiss.

In the distance, fireworks crackled in the sky and illuminated his chiseled features in myriad colors. Her heart beat along with the loud noise.

He stiffened but didn't push her away. She pulled back an inch and felt his hot breath on her cheek. "It's all right."

"The cannons," he murmured against her lips.

Cannons? As a soldier, he must have been exposed to repeated artillery fire. Was he reliving a battle?

Her fingers tightened on his shoulders. "Everything is fine. There is no cannon fire. Only fireworks that are part of the show." When he still didn't respond, she caressed his face with trembling fingers. "Just fireworks," she repeated against his lips. "I promise."

He blinked and focused his gaze. "Fireworks?"

"Yes. Look up and see."

He raised his head and slowly let out a deep breath. "Christ." He swiped a hand across his face, then returned his attention to her. "Did I hurt you?"

Her brows lowered. "No. I'm fine."

He was a large, powerful man, and he easily could have harmed her in his distressed state, but her gut had told her she was safe with him, and she couldn't leave him alone to deal with his crisis.

"Tell me the truth," he demanded.

"I am. You didn't harm me in any way. It's you I'm concerned about."

He let out a long breath. "I need to leave."

"It's all right. It's only me. No one else is here," she said.

"You don't understand. I need to leave this place. Now." His tone was harsh.

She knew men disliked displaying weakness of any kind — especially a former army officer like the Duke of Cameron. "I'll help you."

"No." He shook his head. "No one must see."

"No one will. I promise. I'll tell Henry and the others you had to leave." She took his arm, but he remained unmoving.

"You can trust me. Come."

Several seconds passed and she thought he'd ignore her, but then he nodded. Together they began to make their way along the graveled path toward the pavilion.

She glanced at his profile. "If anyone is watching, it will appear as if you are taking me on a stroll through the gardens."

He didn't argue, and she sensed he was still coming out of his episode. What had he witnessed in battle to make him react so violently to the fireworks? Fellow soldiers wounded or dying? Or was he seeing the faces of the enemy soldiers he'd killed? Pity squeezed her heart.

By the pavilion, a thick crowd remained, all talking about Madame Saqui's fascinating show. Many were drunk on the potent Vauxhall punch. No one paid them any notice. Chloe led Michael to where several boats waited. Thankfully, the docks were empty. All the revelers were still enjoying the gardens. She spotted the ferryman who had rowed them across the Thames, the soldier with the wooden leg.

"His Grace is unwell and needs to get back to his carriage quickly," she instructed.

The ferryman took one look at the duke, then exchanged a knowing glance with her. Blessedly he understood. "Aye, miss."

Michael halted beside the boat and turned to her.

"Good evening, Your Grace," she said.

He raised her arm, but rather than kiss the top of her hand, he turned it over to place a warm kiss in the center of her palm. Her body responded instantly—warming and tingling all over. Her breath came short and fast. When he lifted his head, she saw a need so great in the dark depths of his eyes that she sucked in a breath.

"Thank you," he murmured, then turned and stepped into the boat.

Chloe waited until the craft took off down the Thames before her pounding heart settled to a normal beat. She closed her fingers, as if she could capture and hold his kiss in her palm. They'd shared an experience tonight that had brought them closer. It wasn't just physical, but a deeper connection that she would find hard to forget.

She couldn't help but wonder if he experienced the trauma of the war often. It wasn't as if fireworks were a daily form of entertainment in London. But still, what if he'd been alone? Who would have helped him? She ached with an inner pain at the thought of such a strong, powerful man alone and tormented.

Her thoughts were interrupted when an amorous couple wandered onto the docks, seeking a ferryman to take them across the Thames to their waiting carriage.

Chloe returned to the gardens and wove through the boisterous crowd. As soon as she stepped into the supper box, Lady Willowby was upon her. "Where's His Grace?"

Chloe looked the woman straight in the eye. "I saw him on the way to the entrance. He said he had to leave."

"Leave?" The widow's lips puckered with annoyance.

"He mentioned meeting a former soldier he hadn't seen in years." It was the best lie Chloe could concoct on short notice.

Henry waved a hand. "It's understandable. The duke is a war hero, after all. But I say we should enjoy our remaining time in the gardens together." He plucked a glass of arrack punch from a server's tray and offered it to Lady Willowby.

Lady Willowby took the glass, then eyed Henry with renewed interest. A coy smile curled the corners of her painted lips. "A splendid idea, Lord Sefton."

Eliza took Chloe's arm and pulled her aside to whisper in her ear. "Lady Willowby has been in a sour mood ever since the duke disappeared. I suspect she is unaccustomed to being ignored, and she will be out for her next prey. Watch Lord Sefton, my dear. Now that the duke is gone, I fear she will attempt to charm your earl."

Chloe's throat seemed to close up. The notion of Henry with Lady Willowby should bother her, but her thoughts were not where they should be. Rather, she couldn't stop thinking of the troubled duke who would undoubtedly suffer alone for the rest of the evening.

. . .

By the time Michael reached his carriage, his breathing had almost returned to normal and his hands had ceased shaking. He still hadn't fully recovered, but he had enough of his faculties to realize he had made a mess of things tonight.

God, how the hell could he face her after such a humiliating episode?

It had been fireworks.

Just fireworks.

She'd seen him at his weakest, not once, but twice. He'd been recovering from his fit at Bullock's Museum when she'd literally run into him. But tonight she'd witnessed the entire event.

Damn. He hated the weakness, the vulnerability.

The carriage hit a rut in the road and it felt like a gavel struck his temple. The episodes left him weak with a pounding headache. He lifted the tasseled shade of the carriage and breathed in the outside air.

At last the conveyance stopped at his residence. Not bothering to wait for his driver to open the door, Michael climbed out of the carriage and ascended the steps. Before he could knock, the door opened and his father's trusted butler, Hodges, stood there.

"A bottle of whisky. Upstairs. As soon as possible." Michael's voice was curt.

Instead of snapping to attention, the servant's brow furrowed.

"Perhaps Your Grace requires Dr. Grave's services."

"No." Michael's voice was stern at the mention of his

family's physician. "Bring whisky." The last thing he needed was a physician. They were all butchers who would try to bleed him or bring out jars of bloodsucking leeches. Neither would do him any good.

"Very well, Your Grace," Hodges said.

Michael made his way up the grand staircase, into the master's chambers, and shut the door. Humiliation and guilt washed over him. It was bad enough that his father's faithful servants remained in the house, but they'd witnessed his debilitating fits.

If Hodges hadn't worked for his father and brother for years before their deaths, Michael doubted he'd remain in service now. Not for the first time, Michael was grateful his family was not alive to witness his descent into madness.

He knew of soldiers who suffered similar conditions after Waterloo. War sickness, they'd called it. He also knew the result. They were deemed mad, unfit for military service, and ended up in prisons or asylums. Most committed suicide rather than face a lifetime in the harrowing institutions.

God forbid.

He considered opening the door and apologizing to Hodges, then changed his mind. Why bother? The staff had witnessed Michael at his worst and feared him. He could just imagine their whisperings behind his back.

Beware. Here comes the crazed duke.

He tore off his jacket, waistcoat, and cravat, and tossed them heedlessly onto a chair. His sweat-soaked shirt clung to his skin. He pulled it off along with his trousers and collapsed on the bed. His valet knew to stay away at these times.

A bottle of whisky and a glass were quietly delivered by a young servant. The lad had probably drawn the shortest straw among the staff, and he slipped out as silently as he'd entered.

Leaning back on the pillows, Michael poured himself a tumbler of whisky. Weariness enveloped him as he tried to concentrate on the evening's events. In the military, he would meet with his fellow officers at the end of the day. Maps would be spread out across tables and they would analyze and strategize regarding battles they'd fought and those that were planned. How many lives were lost so far? Could anything have been done differently to reduce the casualties? If so, how?

Such painstaking dissection had been ingrained in him from the military. He may no longer be in the army, but old habits were hard to break. After one of his episodes, he'd tried his best to determine what trigger had sent him back to that bloody battlefield, a dark, desperate place that haunted him despite all his efforts.

It was easy to identify tonight's trigger. The fireworks. The blast of cannon fire was not something any soldier could easily forget. Ear deafening and deadly, it resulted in mass casualties and tore limbs from bodies like a ragdoll in a rabid dog's jaws.

If he'd been alone, he had no idea how he'd react, or heaven forbid, if he'd become violent and attack an unsuspecting passerby. He only knew he'd been aided by the most unlikely savior.

Chloe's voice—sweet and calming—had called out to him from the end of a long dark tunnel. He stumbled forward, guided by the melodic voice murmuring words of comfort. Her feather-like touch grazed his cheek and swept his sweat-soaked hair from his forehead. Then the lightest brush of soft lips against his own was like a soothing balm to his tortured soul. He'd forced his eyes to focus and saw understanding in the heart-wrenching tenderness of her gaze.

He gulped the whisky and rested his head against the headboard. Impossible. How could she know his demons?

Then, just as quickly, he'd felt something other than comfort. He'd felt desire. Raw and aching, he'd trembled with the need to take and dominate. To pleasure and possess.

He was supposed to dissuade her from Henry. He knew deep in his bones that she wasn't for the young earl. Michael had always found Chloe Somerton beautiful and desirable—what man wouldn't? But he never expected this consuming need.

Never before had he wanted a woman so badly. But he wanted her to acknowledge her own passion, to come to him *willingly*. If he weren't careful, she'd become an obsession.

He raised his glass to his lips. The alcohol eased his frayed nerves and dulled the exploding sound of fireworks that continued to echo in his brain.

He welcomed the numbing oblivion.

Chapter Eleven

The following afternoon, Chloe slipped out of the house. She knew Eliza would assume she was going to the orphanage to visit Emily, but Chloe had another destination in mind. She walked a block, then hired a hackney and gave the driver directions to the Duke of Cameron's residence.

She pulled the hood of her cloak down to shield her face as she took the steps to the front door. The risk that someone was watching and might recognize her in the bright afternoon sunlight was real, but her need to see Michael outweighed the risks.

She reached for the brass knocker. The door swung open and the duke's butler glared down at her—the same servant who'd thought she was a woman of loose morals who'd visited his master in the middle of the night little more than a week ago.

Before Chloe could speak a word, the butler said in a curt voice, "His Grace is not receiving visitors today."

Chloe refused to be waylaid. "It's a matter of utmost importance."

His lips thinned with irritation. "Perhaps miss did not hear me — "

Chloe pushed past him and stepped into the vestibule.

"Miss!" He shut the door and reached for her arm.

Evading his grasp, she whirled to face him. "I was with the duke last night at Vauxhall Gardens. *I know.*"

The butler hesitated, and a flicker of uncertainty crossed his rigid features.

Just then a heavyset woman of about fifty, carrying a stack of clean and folded linens, turned a corner and entered the vestibule. From the look of her black dress, with its starched white collar and cuffs, and the thick ring of keys at her waist, Chloe surmised she was the housekeeper.

The woman halted and took one look at Chloe before turning to address the butler. "Is anything amiss, Hodges?"

"Yes, Mrs. Smith. This *lady*" — a bright mockery invaded the butler's stare as he emphasized the false title — "insists on seeing His Grace. She claims she was with him at Vauxhall last night."

Mrs. Smith's gaze snapped back to Chloe. "Is that so?"

Chloe cleared her throat and raised her chin. "I witnessed two of the duke's episodes. One at Bullock's Museum and one last night during the fireworks. I helped him return home, and I assure you that I'm here today out of concern, not curiosity."

Chloe held her breath as the housekeeper measured her with a keenly observant eye before her expression eased and she nodded once as if making an important decision. Mrs. Smith handed the stack of linens to the butler and took Chloe's arm. "We are all concerned. His Grace usually has trouble sleeping, sometimes has bouts of melancholy and drinks too much, but he was very bad last night. Even Hodges thought so. Isn't that right?" She glanced at the butler, who stood frozen, his arms full of snowy linens.

"Where is the duke now?" Chloe asked.

"He's in the master's chambers and still abed," Mrs. Smith said.

Chloe's gaze flew to the longcase clock in the corner of the vestibule. "But it's almost three o'clock!"

"We are all worried, miss," the butler said, his voice low. "But we also know better than to disturb His Grace. On the occasion that any of us has tried, we've been very sorry indeed."

Chloe glanced up at the ornate, gilded balustrade and winding staircase that led to the second floor and the bedchambers. "I will see to him."

Mrs. Smith's brow furrowed. "But he's still abed!"

"His welfare is what concerns me, not propriety." Chloe ignored the gaping servants and hurried up the staircase. She strode down the hall, her footsteps silent on the plush Brussels runner. Priceless artwork whirled by as she passed door after door until she reached what she suspected was the master's chambers at the end of the corridor.

She rapped softly and waited. When there was no response, her fingers grazed the handle. She knew entering a man's bedchamber was recklessly improper, but she thrust the thought aside. She'd *seen* him last night. He'd clearly suffered from shock when the fireworks had exploded at the end of Madame Saqui's performance. She'd witnessed the flash of wild grief that had ripped through him…had glimpsed his pain and inner turmoil in the depths of his eyes. In his mind, he'd been transported back to the horrors of battle.

Without further hesitation, she pushed the door open. The room was dim and her eyes took a moment to adjust. A ray of sunlight that penetrated between the nearly closed curtains provided sufficient light to see. It was a purely masculine room with mahogany Chippendale furniture, a plush Oriental carpet, an escritoire in the corner, and a leather chair by the window. But it was the enormous four-poster that dominated the room—a bed large enough to fit a man well over six feet tall—that drew her eye.

The duke lay in the bed, sprawled on his back in a restless sleep. Heart pounding, Chloe tiptoed close and then stopped breathing at the sight of his bare chest. Unable to stop herself, she stared. Ropes of muscle defined his broad shoulders, biceps, and sculpted chest. His skin was bronzed, and she wondered how he exposed himself to the sun. Her knees grew weak as an image of him riding shirtless arose in her mind. A sprinkling of hair trailed down his flat stomach and disappeared beneath the bedclothes that covered the lower half of his body. One long, muscular leg was uncovered where he'd kicked the linens aside. The raw power of his body nearly stole her breath. With a start, she realized that he slept naked and hadn't bothered with a nightshirt. Had he sent his valet scurrying out of the room last night?

She'd never seen a man's naked chest before, but she knew without a doubt, that no one else of her acquaintance could ever compare.

Certainly not Henry.

Michael had the body of a soldier. He appeared strong and muscled from hours of disciplined training. He was no dandy or coxcomb or spoiled aristocrat who'd never known physical labor. Her fingers trembled with the need to touch his flesh, to run her fingers down his chest.

Deep lines slashed between his dark brows, and he tossed on the bed. "Gavin…no…no. Look out!"

Chloe's eyes flew to his face, and a heavy feeling settled low in her stomach at his distress. He was clearly in the throes of a nightmare. Whatever feelings she had for him, desire and anger, her heart ached to see him in pain. She reached out to touch his arm and lowered her voice to a whisper. "Your Grace."

He moved so fast she didn't have a second to breathe.

Her wrist was caught in a powerful grip and she was pulled down and across his chest. He rolled, taking her with him and pinning her beneath him. Engulfed by his weight, she couldn't move an inch.

Her heart slammed against her chest. She was aware of every rigid angle, every powerful muscle, and his hardness pressing between her thighs made her inhale sharply at the contact. His dark visage was fierce and unyielding as he hovered above her, and she experienced a trepidation of fear.

He'd reacted instinctively, like an experienced soldier who'd been threatened.

"Your Grace!" She gasped. "It's Chloe."

He blinked and focused on her face inches from his. "Chloe?"

"Yes…yes. It's me."

His merciless hold on her arms eased. "Why are you here?"

"I…I was worried about you after last night."

His mouth was set in a grim line, his gaze narrowed and determined. "Christ. I could have killed you. Crushed you as easily as a twig. How the hell did you get into my bedchamber?"

"Your butler and housekeeper told me you were still abed."

One dark eyebrow shot upward. "I'm surprised either permitted you to enter here."

"They didn't. I let myself up here."

"Why does that not surprise me?"

His voice lowered to an intimate whisper and she became even more aware of his hardness pressed against the apex of her thighs. The coverlet had fallen aside so that a thin sheet and her own clothing were the only barriers between them.

Sweet Lord. His manhood seemed so…large. She should have been more afraid—any proper female would have been—but Chloe had never been proper, had she? Instead her initial fear ebbed as she lay soft and pliant beneath him. The physical contact stoked a gently burning fire, and she was powerless to stop the wicked thoughts that came to mind. She was wildly curious by nature, and the hushed whispers of the servants and her own married sisters when they thought she wasn't listening had always fascinated her.

She couldn't stop wondering: what would it be like to know the duke intimately. Would he be gentle or demanding or both?

Their gazes locked, and a corner of his lips turned up in a wicked smile as if he sensed what she was thinking. His pupils expanded, black and gold flecks in his eyes. "I suppose I should be grateful for your impetuous nature which led you here. At last, I have you right where I want you."

All her senses heightened because of their position and his heated words. "Let me up. This is indecent." She flattened her ungloved palms against his chest, whether to push him away or to simply touch him, she wasn't certain. His flesh was hot and enticing, and her fingers curled into his muscles and the light sprinkling of hair.

A sizzling, predatory glimmer sparked in his eyes. "You should have thought of that before you entered a bachelor's bedroom."

He shifted, and she felt him even more firmly. Every nerve ending in her body came alive, and liquid warmth surged between her thighs. She struggled to control her raging emotions, the delicious sensations coursing through her veins. "You were having a nightmare. I was merely concerned."

"Why?"

Because I can't stand to see you suffering. Because I've suffered from bad dreams for years. And because your kisses steal my breath and my body hums when you touch me.

She tried to turn her face away, but he gently held her

chin. There was no escaping his probing gaze. She struggled for an answer to his question, something that would pacify him and keep her uncomfortable feelings hidden, but it was too damned difficult with his magnificent body pressed against hers.

"Tell me why?" he insisted once more.

"Because I know that I'm grateful when someone wakes me from a nightmare."

His brow furrowed. "What do you know about bad dreams?"

"More than you think, Your Grace."

"I told you to call me Michael."

"Fine. I entered your chamber because I was worried after last night, Michael. Nothing more."

She wasn't ready to admit the truth to him—that she felt for his suffering—connected with his deep-seated pain. She may have never been in battle, never experienced the deafening blast of cannon fire, but she *had* known the despair of illness and the fear of dying.

He reached up to take a lock of pale hair that had tumbled from her pins. His fingers entwined with the strands, and he caressed it between his thumb and forefinger. She watched, fascinated, and felt the touch like he'd stroked her actual flesh. Her awareness of him escalated. Her eyes dropped to his mouth…to his perfect lips, and she craved his kiss.

"I don't believe you. I think you knew what would happen as soon as you opened my door, as soon as you touched me. I also think you want it as badly as I do."

Was it true? Deep down she'd known there was more to their verbal sparring. The air sizzled between them whenever they were close.

Had she come here *knowing* what would happen?

Despite their differences—he was a duke, a man who knew about her past and who insisted on meddling with her future. She should hate him, despise his interference, but time had changed her opinion. He was loyal to Henry's father, a deceased man. He didn't have to honor his promise, no one would know, but he took his responsibility seriously. Even though she was the one he was "protecting" Henry from, she grudgingly admired Michael for upholding his vow. She understood loyalty and would do anything to protect her sisters. Perhaps they were similar souls after all.

And like her, he clearly had his demons.

His reaction to Napoleon's gilded carriage at the museum was her first clue. Then the fireworks at the gardens affirmed her thoughts. And today, when she came to check on him, he was in the throes of a nightmare. What she'd told him was true. She knew all about bad dreams that left her reeling with shame and guilt and a hopeless despair.

Logic dictated she stay away from the Duke of Cameron. But all reason flew from her head whenever he was near. An undeniable magnetism had been building between them from the first moment they'd met. And when they touched, when he kissed her, she forgot her well-laid plans and could think only of the passionate escape she found in his arms.

"I promise you won't regret it, Chloe." He raised her chin with his fingers, allowing her to see the fierce hunger and his raw need. His smoldering gaze lowered to her mouth, and she licked her lips in anticipation of his kiss. Only he didn't oblige her. He traced her bottom lip with a fingertip, a slow, sensual movement that made her lips part. "I was never able to properly kiss you last night."

How could she resist him? She'd wanted him to kiss her last evening. She'd hoped it was only the spell cast by the romantic setting of the gardens—the hidden paths and sheltering arbors, the fragrant scent of the flowering bushes, and the soft cast of the lamplight, but the truth was, her need was no different today.

Only now she wanted it more, craved his kiss desperately…

His head lowered, and she met him halfway. His firm lips were caressing and coaxing, generously giving and selfishly taking all at the same time. She sighed into his kiss, gripped his powerful biceps, then wrapped her arms around his back. Smooth muscles rippled beneath her fingers. Her lips parted of their own accord, and she met his tongue in a wild swirl of desire. He tasted of danger and the delicious secrets of mysterious sexual pleasure. A tantalizing combination.

His hand cupped her breasts and her nipples instantly hardened beneath her gown. His lips lowered to graze her neck then trailed down to place heated kisses to her bodice. When he licked the tops of her breasts above her bodice, she arched up to offer herself to his mouth. His fingers dipped into her bodice to graze her nipple, and she moaned. The teasing touch made her wild, made her forget everything but the stroke of his skillful touch.

"From the first time I saw you, I've wanted you naked beneath me. I want to bury myself deep inside you. I want to lavish you with pleasure with my hands and mouth. And I want your hands and mouth on me."

Sweet heaven. Excitement coursed through her veins at his erotic words. He spoke like a soldier, a man in command. But she was far from in control of her own emotions. Her body cried out for his touch, and her resistance dissipated beneath the onslaught of his skillful kisses.

He lifted his head, and a predatory glimmer sparked in his eyes. "I burn to be inside you, but I'd never force you. If you don't want the same, then you have to leave now. It's your choice."

The raw hunger in his eyes sent a burst of warmth through her. Chloe wanted the security of marriage, but she wanted this man even more. Perhaps she was truly wicked and never meant to be a lady. Or perhaps her scandalous past could never be forgotten and had already carved her future in stone. All she knew was that her body ached for everything he'd promised. She wanted him, more than she wanted air to breathe. He was right—she'd known all along that she'd wanted to experience him, hadn't she? It was as inevitable as the stars and the moon.

Despite a strong impulse to glimpse down at his nakedness, she kept her eyes on his face. Reaching up, she traced his jaw. "I choose to stay."

A flicker of surprise crossed his face before it was replaced with a look of pure male satisfaction. "I'll try to go slow, but my desire for you is consuming."

He swooped down to kiss her. She relished his fierceness, knowing he wanted her so badly. His fingers worked the top fastenings of her gown and pushed the fabric down to reveal her breasts. Her nipples tightened from the cool air.

"My God," he hissed. "Your skin is so fair."

His large hands cupped her breast and his hot mouth closed around her nipple. She cried out as deep spirals of pleasure radiated down to her toes. He tasted her with long, leisurely licks. Her body arched wantonly toward his mouth, and her fingers buried in the thick strands of his dark hair. She drowned in sensations as he sucked and kneaded one breast, then moved to the other. He drove her wild, and she'd never imagined her breasts could be so sensitive to another's touch.

He raised the hem of her skirt, his fingers trailing up her silk stockings and halting where her garter met skin. Her clothing was bunched at her waist. She tensed in anticipation of his calloused hand on her flesh, then he touched her *there*.

Chloe moaned. His skillful fingers aroused her and built her excitement slowly. Then he slipped a finger inside her. She felt her wetness bloom and nothing could have stopped her hips from meeting the slow, rhythmic strokes of his finger. When he stroked against the sensitive nub at the apex of her thighs, her head fell back and she cried out.

He lowered his lips to the shell of her ear. "I want to erase the memory of all your prior lovers."

Her mind struggled to comprehend, but the tip of his finger circled her woman's flesh and all thoughts shattered beneath an unimaginable pleasure. He dipped a finger inside, then withdrew to stroke and tease until she was writhing beneath his hand. The pleasure built to a fevered pitch. She needed a release that she knew only he could provide.

He ravished her lips, then trailed his mouth down the column of her throat. He kissed and licked her flesh like it was forever.

Impossible. He didn't want her forever, and she didn't expect it. One afternoon of heated pleasure would have to last her a lifetime.

He shifted and tugged, and the sheet slid to the floor. She caught a glimpse of his manhood—thick, long, and hard. She felt him then, all of him, pressed against her sensitive flesh. She barely had time to wonder before he thrust deep inside her. She cried out at the invading sharp pain.

He froze, his body rigid, his muscles tensing above her. "My God," he hissed through clenched teeth. "You can't be a virgin."

She shook her head from side to side on the pillow. "It doesn't matter. Please don't stop."

Something shifted in him and he tensed. She sensed a battle of restraint in every hard muscle. Her body began to ache for the erotic pleasure he'd promised her. Desperate for release, she wrapped her legs around his waist and squeezed her inner muscles.

"Damn," he hissed. "You're so tight."

At last he began to move, slow rhythmic thrusts until her body accepted his fullness. A burning, then aching sensation leaped to life within her. Soon the hot sliding friction aroused her to a fevered pitch. She relished the weight of his body, his muscular chest brushing against her own sensitive breasts, the scent of his skin, and the pulsing fullness of him inside her. She ran her hands up his muscular arms and buried her fingers in his hair.

He took her mouth as he increased the tempo of his thrusts. "I've never seen anyone as beautiful in the throes of passion as you."

The pleasure built and built. Her hips arched off the mattress to meet his thrusts. Then he reached between their bodies to stroke her flesh. She cried out as she was hurled beyond and her body exploded in a fiery climax.

"Chloe!" With a hoarse groan, he threw his head back and withdrew from her body. He shook, his face softening with an unexpected vulnerability, as he reached his own climax and his seed spurt across the linens.

He rolled to the side and pulled her into his arms. Chloe lay pressed against him, breathing heavily. She wanted to close her eyes and rest her head on his chest. He was a man who made her feel deliciously ravished, yet protected and safe at the same time.

Then he rose on an elbow and glared down at her. "Why didn't you tell me you were a virgin?"

Chapter Twelve

At the harshness of Michael's tone, Chloe's lashes fluttered open. "You assumed I was experienced. I just never corrected you."

"Why the hell not?"

She blinked at the face of his anger. "Would you have believed me? You know I've lied about my past for years. You've reminded me of it on more than once occasion."

He had the good sense to look apologetic. "Forgive me. Clearly, I was wrong. But you should have told me. I don't ruin innocents, and I *never* proposition them to be my mistress. God, the way I took you. I should have been gentler."

She reached up to stroke his jaw. "It was perfect and I wouldn't change anything about it."

He looked at her curiously. "You're amazing. I'll never forget the shared passion between us. But I must warn you that I still cannot offer marriage."

Her heart hammered at his admission. She knew the reason. Her past ensured she'd never be duchess material, but the question came out regardless. "Why? Because I am a thief?"

"No. I won't marry anyone. Ever."

She eyed him speculatively. "You're a duke. You must marry and produce the next heir."

"No, I don't. I don't give a damn about the title. It can go to a distant relative for all I care."

She didn't fully understand. All titled men knew of their duty to marry and produce an heir. Did he believe his episodes prevented him from having a wife? It was a foolish thought. Plenty of young ladies would be willing to marry a duke—regardless of sanity, age, hair, or even teeth, for the chance to be a duchess. And Michael's striking looks turned ladies' heads when he walked into a room.

"Even though I cannot marry, you must know that Henry isn't for you."

Her eyes narrowed slightly. She'd known this, of course. She would never have been with Michael if she intended to continue to encourage Henry's pursuit. But the fact that Michael had even brought it up made her angry. Was his opinion of her so low?

Apparently so. A man did not have to a like a woman to bed one.

Sourness settled in her gut.

He rose and went to a basin and returned with a clean cloth. Sitting at her hip, his hands were infinitely gentle as he skimmed her skin and cleansed her and the linens of the evidence of their lovemaking. When he finished, he brushed his lips against hers with tenderness that melted her misgivings.

"If I had known, I would have taken you slowly and leisurely and with infinite care."

Her heart was a slippery slope, and he was playing havoc with her emotions. He stood and returned the cloth to the basin, and she leaned up on elbows and watched the play of muscles on his back and buttocks. Without a stitch of clothing, he was a magnificent sight.

She sat up as he returned to the bed. She was still in her dress. She smoothed the skirts and righted her bodice. Her satin shoes had fallen off and dropped to the floor. Her hair was disheveled, and she righted the blond tresses as best as she could. "I must look a mess."

He sat beside her on the bed. "You look lovely."

She felt her face heat at the intensity of his look, and she felt suddenly shy. The emotion made no sense after what they'd just shared in his bed, but nonetheless, it was there. She wanted to reach up and brush the silky, dark hair that fell across his forehead, but her fingers clenched in her lap. He was a complex man, a powerful duke who could be confident and arrogant, yet a remarkably gentle and considerate lover. She found herself fascinated.

The need to learn more about him arose. What could cause this strong man to have nightmares? "You said a name while you slept. Who's Gavin?"

He stiffened and remained silent for a while. She thought he wouldn't tell her, but then he finally spoke. "Gavin was Henry's father, the former Lord Sefton. He was a childhood friend from Eton and then Oxford. He died saving my life in battle."

"I'm sorry." She couldn't imagine the trauma of watching your friend die…a friend who'd sacrificed his life to save hers. She'd struggle with the guilt for the rest of her life. Perhaps that was what was behind his fits…a deep-seated guilt that he'd survived rather than Henry's father.

"We had sustained heavy casualties from the French soldiers and artillery. We finally thought the worst was over, then I glimpsed an enemy solider stealthily approach from behind. Before I could act, Gavin pushed me aside and took a bullet in his chest. I pursued and killed the Frenchman, but it was too late. Gavin died. He'd carried a letter asking for me to look after his only son."

Chloe's heart ached for him. He'd always feel protective of Henry. The promise he'd made to a dying friend who'd taken a bullet for him wasn't something a soldier could ignore. And knowing the Duke of Cameron, he felt the responsibility even more than the average military officer. "Last night at Vauxhall Gardens when the fireworks exploded, you were reminded of the war?"

"Yes."

"And the first time I met you at Bullock's Museum, when we saw Napoleon's carriage, you had an episode as well?"

He nodded. "I'm powerless to stop the fits. Anything can trigger them, and I'm taken back to the war, to the battle where I lost my best friend. I've had difficulty sleeping since my return."

Chloe's nightmares weren't of bloody battlefields, but of sickness, poverty, and running from constables in dark, damp alleys. Both had the same effect. Neither of them could sleep peacefully through the night.

"You helped me last night. I'm grateful," he said.

"Anyone would have done the same."

"No, you're wrong. You are no wallflower, Chloe, or a delicate miss. Your past has shaped you and made you different from all the other debutantes. It's made you special and I admire it."

He admired her past? *Heavens*. She wondered if he could hear her wildly beating heart.

She patted the bed beside her. "Lie down."

A corner of his lips turned upward. "I'm more than happy to oblige you, but I think you'd be too sore."

Her cheeks heated. "Not for that. I have an idea to help ease your tension. Now lie down on your stomach."

"Your wish is my command." He flipped over.

He had to have the most perfect backside. She rose on her knees beside him and began to stroke his scalp. Her fingers stroked his temples and kneaded the muscles at the base of his neck and across his shoulders. He flexed and she watched the play of muscles across his back and buttocks.

He groaned. She felt his breathing relax and the tenseness in his shoulders ease. They sat in silence as she soothed his stress with her fingers. His breathing grew deeper until his eyes closed and he became drowsy. Soon he slept. She watched him for several moments. His face was relaxed and he appeared younger.

She had no regrets. One afternoon of passion may have changed her forever, but she refused to allow it to alter her future.

She grabbed her reticule and quietly slipped out.

• • •

Michael woke feeling better rested than he had in over a year. He had slept a deep, dreamless sleep free of horrific nightmares of shadowy battlefields and bloodcurdling screams. Chloe's smooth, stroking fingers on his neck, across his shoulders, and down his back had released much of the tension he'd been carrying.

If only a cure to his condition were that simple.

He reached across the bed. Empty. His eyes flew open. She'd gone. He knew not to be surprised or disappointed, but nonetheless, his chest tightened with an unknown emotion.

What did he expect? She couldn't stay. She'd be ruined.

She already was.

Christ. She'd been a virgin. Never in his wildest dreams had he believed she was sexually innocent. He would have bet all the fortune of the dukedom that she was experienced, and he would have lost. She possessed an innate sensuality that made a man think of tangled sheets and earthy sex. He'd been determined to bed her, to make her his mistress, only to learn that she was innocent and pure.

He was a rogue, a blackguard. He didn't go around seducing innocents or seeking to make them his lovers. He should feel remorseful, but the truth was he was more shaken than regretful. Now that he'd tasted her passion, would he ever be satisfied by another? He screwed his eyes shut as heated memories returned in a rush.

God...the silken softness of her skin, her golden hair spread across his pillow, and her throaty moans of pleasure had driven him over the edge, until he'd lost all control and had thrust inside her wet, welcoming body. He reached for the pillow beside him and inhaled. Her unique scent—lemongrass and lavender—lingered. He rubbed a hand down his face. Another scent—female arousal—clung to his hands.

He wanted her again. Badly.

But he couldn't bind her to his side. She'd been a virgin, and he grudgingly admitted that she was right to demand marriage. Had he been a cruel bastard to keep her from the likes of men like Henry when he couldn't offer her what she deserved?

No, Henry wasn't for her. Of that he was certain. But *he* wasn't for her, either. The all too familiar feelings of anger and frustration roiled in his gut.

He'd been in bad shape after the fireworks. He owed Chloe a debt of gratitude for helping him get home unnoticed. He'd still been suffering the effects of his latest episode when she'd showed up in his bedchamber over twelve hours afterward.

He'd braced himself for her pity—even her disgust—when he'd told her about the death of his best friend in battle, but to his amazement it hadn't come. In its place had been an instant of connection...of understanding...as if she'd experienced an emotional wound herself—a harrowing event that had caused her great pain.

Could it be true?

He knew so little about her past. Yes, he'd seen her

pickpocket with startling ease. But why had she done it? He'd always assumed that she needed money—like many of the struggling lower classes in the city—but that explanation didn't entirely make sense, because her sisters had owned a print shop. They hadn't been wealthy, but neither had they been impoverished. So why had she done it? What was the reason behind her thievery?

Chloe Somerton was as complex as she was fascinating.

His opinions about her were changing. She wasn't just a cold-blooded woman, a former pickpocket who was after Henry for his title and fortune. Most shockingly, she hadn't feared his madness last night, but she'd taken care to see him home and had returned the next day to check on him.

He could have hurt her last night during the fireworks. He could have hurt her when she caught him unawares today and woke him. It would have been easy to break the delicate bones in her wrist, or heaven forbid, to snap her neck. His jaw clamped tight. Thank goodness he'd recognized her before his battle-hardened instincts had kicked in.

She'd ended up beneath him instead. Soft, sweet, and oh so tempting.

He couldn't marry anyone, not when he was suffering this war sickness. Not when anything could trigger his slow descent to insanity, whether it be a former French tyrant's carriage in a museum or fireworks at Vauxhall Gardens.

Humiliation and anger raged within him, and he clenched his jaw until it ached. He was damaged. A broken man. He refused to subject a wife and children to his darkest demons. But he believed, more than ever before, that Henry was no match for Chloe. After what they shared in his bed, she must know this as well.

She *had* to know.

But there would be other men. Could he do it? Could he let Chloe go and watch her marry another?

Chapter Thirteen

Chloe was careful to return through the servants' entrance of Huntingdon's town house. Muscles she hadn't known existed were sore and she moved slowly. She'd always been impetuous, but she didn't regret a moment of the afternoon. As long as she lived, the memory of the pleasure she'd found in Michael's arms would remain vivid in her mind. She knew she'd always compare other men to him and they'd fall short.

Michael had been right. She'd known what would happen between them as soon as she'd dared step foot inside his bedchamber. From the beginning, the attraction between them had simmered and grown until neither of them could resist the pull. She recognized it now. Deep down, she'd desired him as much as he'd wanted her.

There could be serious consequences if the truth became known. Eliza and Huntingdon would demand the Duke of Cameron propose marriage. And for that reason, Chloe would take the secret to her grave.

She didn't want to marry a man who had to be forced to the altar. She wanted to marry, yes, but she wanted a man who *wanted* her. The duke had made his intentions clear—whether it was because he thought himself ill or he truly didn't want a wife—the result was the same.

Chloe would be no man's mistress.

She breathed a sigh of relief as she made her way through the kitchen and connecting hallways unnoticed. She desperately wanted a bath and planned to ring for her maid, Alice, as soon as she reached her bedchamber. Her footsteps were silent on the carpet runner as she walked to the main part of the house and the stairs leading up to the second floor. Her slipper touched the first step when she heard her name.

"Miss Chloe?"

Chloe whirled, her hand clutching the ornate banister. "Alice? You scared me half to death."

"Sorry, my lady. Let me see to you upstairs."

As soon as Chloe's bedchamber door closed, Alice asked, "What happened last night at Vauxhall Gardens? I overheard Lady Huntingdon say the duke had to leave early." It had been Alice's evening off, and Chloe hadn't been able to explain.

"He did. But not for the reason I told everyone."

"You were with him, weren't you?"

"I was."

Alice shot a brown upward. "And Lord Sefton?"

"Was watching Madame Saqui's performance with the rest of the group."

Her maid shot her a speculative look. "You had a secret rendezvous with the duke last night, didn't you?"

Chloe shook her head. "No. It wasn't like that last night. I helped him then, but I saw him again this afternoon."

Alice looked at her knowingly, then nodded. Thankfully, her maid never judged her. "I never thought Lord Sefton was a good match for you. You are too intelligent and strong-willed for him."

"Neither is the Duke of Cameron. He had a seizure of

sorts when the fireworks went off. I believe it took him back to the war and the horrors of cannon fire."

Alice was silent for several seconds. "I've heard of soldiers returning from battle with illnesses of the mind. My cousin's husband suffered ill effects after Waterloo."

"What happened to him?"

"He went to an asylum. Everyone thought him mad. Last I heard he hung himself."

Oh God. Chloe tired to swallow the lump that rose in her throat. Could that happen to Michael? How bad was his condition? She'd witnessed two events—both deeply unsettling. What if there were many others, even more debilitating? His servants had said he'd go for days without leaving the house. What if he was a danger to himself?

She refused to believe it.

"Our own cook's husband also experienced something similar since the war. Not long ago, he woke up screaming from nightmares. Shook the servants' quarters and scared me something fierce," Alice said.

A question formed on Chloe's lips when a knock sounded on the door. Alice opened it to find the butler in the doorway. "There is a gentleman caller here to see you, miss," he said.

For a heart-stopping moment, Chloe thought Michael had followed her home. Did he feel honor bound to do the right thing after all? Her mind spun as she clutched the bedpost for support. Good grief, was he here to speak with Huntingdon?

"Who is it?" she said in a raw voice.

The butler watched her, a peculiar expression on his normally impassive face. Chloe resisted the urge to reach up and smooth her hair. She'd been careful to fix her hair in the hackney ride home, but without a looking glass who knew how successful she'd been?

"Lord Sefton. I put him in the drawing room."

Chloe managed a weak smile. "Thank you."

Her relief was short-lived and her heart began pounding anew in her chest. Henry was here? A feeling of dread swept over her. She hadn't thought of him since she'd left Vauxhall Gardens last evening. She certainly hadn't thought of him when she went to the duke's home this afternoon.

She didn't want to see him. Not now. Not after the exquisite afternoon she'd spent in Michael's arms. She had to turn him down, but how? She couldn't tell him the truth. She'd have to explain how she felt about him, that she thought fondly of him, but as a friend.

She took a deep breath. Best get the unpleasant business over with. "Please inform Lord Sefton I'll be there shortly."

Chloe waited until the butler closed the door before addressing Alice. "Quick. Help me change my clothes and repair my hair."

Half an hour later, Chloe opened the drawing room door. Henry was looking out the window at the gardens below. Arms folded across his back, he looked handsome…and young. At the rustling of her skirts, he turned. His lips curled in a brilliant smile as he approached and took her hand. In her haste, she'd forgotten her gloves and he brushed his lips across her knuckles. He must have given his own gloves to the butler, and his fingers were smooth and cool, so different from the calloused, powerful hands of another.

"Chloe, you look lovely as always. Thank you for seeing me. I was told you'd returned from your afternoon visit to the orphanage."

"Yes," she lied. "There is a sick child I've grown very attached to. I look forward to visiting Emily as much as she anticipates my visits."

Henry's brown furrowed. "The orphan is ill? Perhaps you shouldn't see her. You could contract her illness."

"It's not like that. No one who has cared for her has become ill."

"Still, I worry for you. I admire your charitable activities, but there are plenty of healthy orphans who could benefit from a lady's visit. I suggest you visit others."

Annoyance prickled her spine. Didn't he realize how much Emily meant to her? They shared a bond and Chloe wasn't about to let anyone dissuade her from seeing the child.

If she married Henry, he'd have a say in all her activities. He could prohibit her from visiting Emily. He may mean well, but she couldn't imagine not seeing Emily. Her hands twisted in her skirts.

Henry's expression grew serious. "I couldn't stop thinking of you after last night at Vauxhall Gardens. Our time alone was too limited."

His complexion was pale, not tanned from spending hours marching outside with fellow soldiers. His skin was smooth, without the distinguished fine lines around his eyes that came from worldly experience. He was pretty, not strong or virile or ruggedly handsome, and she knew that she could only think of him as a friend, never a lover.

Not for the first time, she wondered what Henry would think of her if he knew the truth about her past. Surely he would cease his pursuit. He'd think she was just like her father, the infamous forger and thief. He wouldn't be wrong, would he? She'd often feared the tainted blood that ran through her veins.

What would Michael do if he knew the truth…the entire truth? She hadn't just stolen trinkets and handed them to Mr. Allenson at the apothecary. She'd had to go elsewhere for the coin the chemist had required.

After hearing Michael's story and learning the extent of his tragedy and that his best friend gave his life to save his, she believed he'd react differently to her past.

Either way, she knew what she had to do. She may be unsure about her future, but she couldn't lie to Henry. He deserved better than to believe there could be a future between them.

Henry took her hand. "Chloe, you must know how I feel about you, and I sense you feel the same about me."

Her mouth felt like old paper, dry and dusty. She needed to tell him...had to tell him that things had changed for her. "Henry, I must tell you—"

He placed a finger to her lips. "Shh. I know."

She blinked. "You do?"

"I know you feel the same, and I plan on speaking privately with Huntingdon."

There was only one reason for Henry to speak privately with her brother-in-law: he planned to ask for her hand in marriage. Even though she was over the age of consent, without her father's presence, Henry thought to act honorably by speaking with Huntingdon.

Her stomach dropped. "No! That's not what I wanted to say. There's someone—"

Just then the door to the drawing room opened and Eliza stood in the doorway. "Lord Sefton! What a wonderful surprise. We were just speaking of you."

Chloe chewed on her lower lip. *Of all the rotten timing.*

"I hope it was in a positive light," Henry said.

"Of course," Eliza said, her green gaze glittering with excitement. "Huntingdon and I are hosting a small dinner party Friday evening and would love for you and the duke to attend. A few other guests will be present as well."

Henry clasped a hand to his chest. "I'd be honored."

"Splendid," Eliza said. "Now I'm afraid I must take Chloe with me for an appointment to Madame Adalene."

Chloe stared. "Madame Adalene? The dressmakers?"

"Of course. Tell me you haven't forgotten?" Eliza said. "We need new ball dresses for Lady Rosewood's upcoming ball."

It had been the last thing on Chloe's mind.

Henry's eyes bathed Chloe in admiration as he bowed. "I know better than to keep a lady from her modiste. Until Friday then."

This couldn't go on. Henry mustn't speak with Eliza and Huntingdon. Somehow she'd have to find a way to speak with him privately and explain.

Chloe forced a smile as she looked up at him with an effort. "I shall look forward to it."

. . .

"I plan on asking Lord Huntingdon for Miss Chloe's hand in marriage."

Michael's gaze snapped to Henry. He had been pouring himself a glass of brandy in his library when his butler had announced Henry's arrival. Michael set the glass down on the sideboard. "What the hell are you talking about?"

Henry wasn't put off by his tone. Rather he smiled with genuine happiness. "I went to visit Miss Chloe later this afternoon."

"You did?" A sudden thin chill hung on the edge of his words, but Henry appeared oblivious.

"I told her I wanted to speak with Huntingdon privately."

Bloody hell. "What did she say?"

A wistful look crossed Henry's face. "She was lovely as usual, in a pale yellow gown that reminded me of a field of buttercups during a lovely spring—"

"Henry," Michael snapped. "What did she say?"

"Lady Huntingdon interrupted our conversation. We are invited to a small gathering at their home Friday evening. I hope to speak officially with Huntingdon about Chloe's hand in marriage."

Every nerve in Michael's body tensed and his fists balled

at his sides. Jealousy clawed at his gut like talons. She hadn't said a word. He understood that Chloe couldn't confess to an illicit tryst in his bed merely hours ago, but she could have told Henry she was no longer interested in his courting.

Or did she still intend to lure Henry into the marriage trap?

Hell.

One afternoon of pleasure haunted him. When had things become so damned complicated? From the beginning, his goals had been simple: to look after Henry and honor a debt to his father. Then Chloe Somerton had shown up at the museum, and his world had tilted on its axis. He'd wanted her out of Henry's life and into his own bed. He'd misjudged her and thought she was experienced when it came to men. He never believed she'd been innocent. A nagging guilt rose within him when it came to *both* Henry and Chloe.

He needed to do better for Sefton's son. But how, when he'd taken Chloe and still had a burning desire, an aching need, for another kiss?

He wanted more from her—he wanted everything.

Unthinkable.

She deserved marriage, and he could never, ever commit. He picked up the discarded brandy, threw back his head, and swallowed its contents.

Henry eyed him curiously. "Are you well?"

"Never better."

Henry's shoulders eased a notch. "You will agree to go to Lady Huntingdon's gathering Friday evening, won't you?"

Michael clenched the empty crystal as he reached for the decanter. "Don't worry. I won't let you down."

Chapter Fourteen

The following morning, Chloe woke later than usual. Memories of her heated afternoon with the duke had invaded her dreams. She struggled to push them aside. Nothing could come of their time together, no matter how often she relived the velvet warmth of his kiss or the tantalizing caresses of his calloused hands on her skin.

The bedchamber door opened, and Alice stepped inside. After dressing, Chloe hurried to the breakfast room where she nibbled on buttered toast and sipped a cup of tea, then called for the butler to summon a carriage. Fifteen minutes later, Chloe arrived at the orphanage and hurried up the steps. She was late, and young Emily would surely be waiting. Her footsteps sounded off the worn floorboards as she rushed down the hall to the room the younger girls shared.

Mrs. Porter waylaid Chloe just outside the room. Her face was flushed, and her ample bosom heaved in her bodice. "Emily's health is declining," she stated abruptly.

Chloe's nerves tensed. "Has the orphanage doctor seen the child?"

"Dr. Mason was here yesterday. She's not improving, and he fears she will not. I should also inform you that Mr. Whitleson has returned."

"I'd like to speak with him about Emily."

Mrs. Porter nodded. "Follow me."

Chloe was led into an office she'd never seen before. Mrs. Porter had always met her in the vestibule or was busy seeing to the numerous daily duties that were part of running the orphanage and caring for the children.

Mr. Whitleson, it appeared, acted in a much different capacity. Chloe scanned the bookshelves then spotted a pair of wooden chairs situated before an oak desk. Papers cluttered the surface of the desk, and Chloe suspected they had to do with the business aspects of the orphanage.

Mr. Whitleson sat behind the desk. A gaunt man with wiry salt-and-pepper hair, he had small dark eyes. He stood as soon as the women entered the room.

Mrs. Porter made the introductions. "This is Miss Somerton. I've told you about her visits."

"Ah, yes." Mr. Whitleson came around the desk. "Please have a seat, Miss Somerton." He motioned to one of the wooden chairs, and Chloe sat and smoothed her skirts. Mr. Whitleson sat behind his desk. Something flickered in the depths of his dark eyes as he studied her intently. The hairs on Chloe's nape rose, but she forced herself to smile serenely and meet his gaze.

The questionable look disappeared. "May I offer you refreshment?" Mr. Whitleson asked.

"No, thank you."

He motioned to Mrs. Porter, and the woman left the room.

Mr. Whitleson sat back in his chair. "You are related to the Earls of Huntingdon and Vale?"

"Yes, they are married to my sisters."

He rubbed his chin with a thumb and forefinger as he

looked at her curiously. "I met Lord and Lady Huntingdon at the theater a while back. You look familiar. Perhaps you accompanied them?"

She didn't think so, but she couldn't be certain. Drury Lane was always crowded. A frisson pierced her spine. Was it possible she'd run into him in the past? But where? At the print shop? The apothecary? Or worse…at the Seven Sins brothel when she'd met with Madame Satine?

No. That was highly unlikely. The proprietress had always been careful to meet Chloe in her private chambers away from the brothel's paying customers. Chloe would then trade her stolen wares for coin.

Chloe forced herself to relax. She was acting paranoid. The chances were slim to none that he would recognize her even if he'd glimpsed her coming or leaving the brothel. It had been years. She was no longer wearing a shabby dress, with her hair tied in a simple bow at her nape. She was dressed in a fine gown, and Alice had styled her hair in a sleek chignon. A string of simple pearls adorned her throat. No one would suspect the sister-in-law of two powerful and well-respected nobles had picked pockets in her youth and conducted business with an infamous brothel owner.

"It's likely you saw me at the theater," she said. "My sister and I enjoy Drury Lane, especially the Shakespearean performances."

He nodded in satisfaction. "The cast was performing *Hamlet* that night."

She gifted him with another smile, one that had never failed to charm. "I asked to speak with you to discuss one of the young children here."

"Ah, yes. Emily Higgins. Mrs. Porter told me you are fond of the girl."

"I was told her health is not improving."

"It's true. Dr. Mason's prognosis is not a positive one."

Despair settled in Chloe's stomach. "If there is anything the child needs, please let—"

"Thank you, that's not necessary. Dr. Mason has increased the dose and frequency of her tonic. He believes it is her last chance for improvement."

Her last chance? Chloe's nerves tensed. It had to work. The alternative was unthinkable. She pushed back her chair and stood. "I should like to see Emily now."

He stood. "Of course. But a word of advice, Miss Somerton. It's best if you prepare yourself for the worst. I've learned from my time here that miracles rarely happen."

• • •

Miracles rarely happen.

No one knew that more than Chloe. But she could still pray for one.

Chloe approached Emily's bedside. Black hair streamed across the white pillow, and the child's small face was pale and angelic. Emily's eyes fluttered open and she smiled when Chloe came close.

"Emily, sweetheart, how do you feel today?" Chloe asked.

"Not so well, Miss Chloe. I can hear the other children playing outside, but the doctor says I can't join them."

Chloe swallowed the lump that rose in her throat. "I can carry you outside if you wish. We can watch them together."

Emily shook her head. "I think it would be worse to watch and not join them." There was longing in her voice that nearly broke Chloe's heart.

Chloe wanted to scream at the injustice of it all. "Then I shall sit and read to you." She pulled up the wooden chair, settled the book on her lap, and opened to the page where she'd stopped reading on her last visit.

"I'd like that. But I don't know if the big man would like

a princess story."

Chloe's eyes snapped to Emily's. "What big man?"

"The one standing behind you."

Chloe whirled around to find Michael a few steps behind her. Her hand fluttered to her chest. Where on earth had he come from? And how could such a large man move so stealthily? "What are you doing here?"

The corner of his lips twitched. "It's a pleasure to see you as well."

Chloe stood and the book thumped to the floor.

"Who is he?" Emily asked behind her.

Chloe cleared her throat and turned to Emily. The child was leaning on her elbows and looking questioningly at both of them. "Emily, this is His Grace, the Duke of—"

"Michael. My name is Michael." He stepped close to the bedside and crouched down to offer Emily his hand. "How do you do, Emily?"

Emily tentatively reached out. Her tiny fingers were pale and ridiculously fragile in his big hand. "You're the tallest and biggest person I've ever seen."

He smiled. "You're the smallest person I've seen in a long time."

Emily's lips curled in a hint of a smile. "Are you Miss Chloe's friend?"

Dark eyes gazed up at Chloe before returning to Emily. "I am."

He'd called her his friend when there was so much more between them. She no longer considered him a cold, distant man who wanted to keep her away from his ward.

"It's nice to have a friend," Emily said. "I'm no longer allowed to play with the other girls."

"That must be hard."

Emily shrugged a slight shoulder. "Miss Chloe brings me pretty pictures of the outdoors." She motioned to Chloe's lithographs displayed on a wood shelf above the bed.

Michael stood to study the artwork. "They're lovely. I confess that I didn't know she was an artist." He looked at Chloe, and her skin tingled beneath his stare.

"Her father was a great painter," Emily said with pride.

"So I've heard."

Chloe held her breath. She expected a disapproving retort or piercing stare, but instead he continued to look at her with renewed interest...as if her family's past wasn't scandalous, but her artwork was to be admired.

"Miss Chloe also reads to me. Do you like stories about princesses and princes?" Emily asked.

Michael nodded. "When I was a boy my favorite story was about a prince fighting a dragon."

"A fire-breathing dragon?" Emily asked.

The corner of Michael's lips tilted in a charming grin. "Is there any other kind?"

Emily's eyes widened in her oval face. "What did they fight over?"

"The princess."

"Did the prince win?"

"Always. He killed the dragon and saved the princess."

"How did he do it?" Emily asked.

"It's quite a story. Do you want to hear it?"

"Oh yes," Emily said.

Michael spotted a second wooden chair, placed it by Chloe's chair, and sat.

Chloe watched, amazed, as he took his time with the child. His voice was animated, his tale entertaining, and when he acted out the part where the prince killed the dragon, both Emily and Chloe hung on his every word. Never in Chloe's wildest dreams would she have thought the Duke of Cameron would have taken the time to tell a sick, orphaned child a fairy tale. But then, she never anticipated he'd show up here in the first place. Which led her to another question: there were dozens of orphanages in London, so how had he found her here?

An emotion tugged Chloe's chest. She fought it, knowing her feelings were treading on dangerous ground. Her physical attraction to him was understandable. But an emotional attraction was perilous.

Sunlight from an overhead window glinted off his dark hair and emphasized his handsome profile. He exuded power and dominance that beckoned to a woman's secret desires. But it was more than a physical pull that frightened her—it was his strength of character that tugged at her chest, and his empathy for a sick child. He was a danger to her heart.

When Emily's eyelids began to flutter, Chloe placed a hand on the child's sleeve. "You should rest now."

"But I like Mr. Michael's stories. Will he come back to visit?" Emily implored.

"I don't think—"

"Yes," Michael interrupted. "Not even a fire-breathing dragon could keep me away, Miss Emily."

Emily beamed. "Then it's safe to sleep."

Her eyelids fluttered, and moments later the child was sleeping soundly.

Chloe stood, and Michael followed her out of the room into the dim hall. "What's wrong with Emily?" he asked.

"She suffers from an unexplainable apathy and has difficulty breathing during the slightest activity. The doctor who visits the orphanage has no explanation, but believes her health is slowly declining."

His brows drew downward. "I'm sorry."

"It's unfair to give Emily a promise you don't intend to keep. She's suffered too much disappointment at an early age."

"Who says I plan to break my promise?"

She looked at him in surprise. "You are a duke. Surely you have more pressing matters to attend to than to visit a sick orphan."

"I can't think of a single one."

His words chipped away at her defenses and awoke something deep and profound within her. It was almost as if he *knew* how important Emily was to her, and he'd taken the utmost care with the child. "How did you find me here?" she asked.

"The day at the museum, your sister mentioned you visited an orphanage on Tuesdays and Thursdays. I also overheard you tell Henry in Lady Webster's conservatory."

Had he listened that closely and taken note of her schedule?

"I had no idea which orphanage. This is the third establishment I've been to today," he said.

She stared at him in astonishment. He was a duke, for heavens sake. Had he truly gone through the effort to visit orphanages just to find her? "Why go to the trouble?"

His scrutiny was almost a physical caress. "I needed to see that you're all right today. It was your first time and I wasn't gentle."

Heat rushed to her cheeks at his mention of their passionate afternoon together. *He cares.* "I'm fine." Except she was far from fine. Her emotions were wreaking havoc with her heart—tugging in uncomfortable ways.

He skimmed his forefinger along her cheek. "Now you must answer my question. Why Emily?"

"Pardon?"

"It's obvious you've made an emotional connection with the child. Why not any of the other girls here?"

Her chest tightened. Her immediate response was to lie, but his dark, earnest eyes probed for the truth. Her voice was barely above a whisper. "I was sick as a child as well."

He stood still. "How sick?"

"It started as a cold, but then I developed a cough. Times were difficult when we'd first opened the Peacock Print Shop. What little coal we could afford was used to heat the shop downstairs rather than our living quarters on the second floor. It was a very cold winter, and I'd often climb into bed with Eliza or Amelia to stay warm. I was just shy of thirteen years at the time. Instead of recovering as expected, my cough lingered and lingered. The physician said I had weak lungs."

"You recovered."

She shook her head and turned away. "No, not right away. Eliza had to scrape what little profit the print shop made that first winter to purchase cough tonic for me from the apothecary. The owner, Mr. Allenson, was not a generous soul, and the medicine I required was costly. The cough came and went for over three and a half years, and I still needed the tonic for a long while afterward. I was a financial and emotional drain on my two sisters."

"You can't really believe that."

She looked up at him. "It's true. Eliza worked tirelessly to ensure the print shop was a success. Amelia sold a forgery to help with the first month's rent. I did nothing but cause them worry and cost them coin every time they had to visit the apothecary."

His voice was uncompromising, yet oddly gentle. "You cannot blame yourself. You were only a child at the time and you were ill."

"It doesn't matter. They sacrificed because of me."

He hesitated, searching her face. She felt naked, stripped of her defenses, as if he could see into her soul and discover all her deepest and darkest secrets. "That's why you started stealing, isn't it?"

When she didn't respond, he reached out and shook her arms. "Isn't it?"

It was impossible to escape his scrutiny. "I paid the apothecary owner, Mr. Allenson, with my stolen goods. It still wasn't enough to cover the entire cost, but he would lower the price of the tonic when my sisters would arrive to purchase it. Eliza and Amelia never knew."

The story was partly the truth. She did pay Mr. Allenson, but not with her stolen goods. Mr. Allenson had no use for embroidered handkerchiefs or jeweled clips. He was only interested in money, and that meant Chloe had to find someone who would pay her for the stolen trinkets. She'd found an invaluable resource in Madame Satine, the owner of the infamous Seven Sins brothel, who'd offered her the coins she needed in exchange for the items. The proprietress liked her girls, and she'd give the stolen items to them as gifts. The arrangement may have helped Chloe at the time, but it was also a secret that could ruin her and her sisters.

She could never reveal the *entire* truth to him or to anyone. She felt a deep-seated shame even though she'd done what was necessary to survive.

He gently squeezed her arms. "So your sisters never learned that you picked pockets?"

"No, and I want to keep it that way."

"I shall keep your secret. But you should know your illness was not your fault, and I was wrong to call you a thief. I don't know many who would have had the strength to do what you did to aid your sisters."

She stood still, blank and amazed. Never had she imagined to receive admiration from the Duke of Cameron. For a moment, she wanted to confess *everything,* but she held her tongue.

Insanity. No matter how strong her feelings had grown for this man she must never forget he was a duke and she was the daughter of an art forger. He held the power to ruin her with a single word.

"Now tell me why *you* are here?" she said.

"I wanted to see with my own eyes what you do on Tuesdays and Thursdays."

"You mean you wanted to know if I was telling the truth about my charitable activities."

"I won't deny it. But there's another reason, too. Henry came to see me. He said he visited you and plans to speak with Huntingdon."

Chloe felt her face pale. "I see."

"Do you mean to let him ask for your hand?"

"You mean after what happened between us?"

A crease formed between his brows. "You regret it, then."

"I've stopped living my life by regrets long ago. You needn't worry about Henry. He is not for me, and I shall tell him myself as soon as I am able."

A flicker of emotion crossed his features—Satisfaction? Relief?—but it was gone and the familiar mask of confidence descended. "Good. Because despite my guilt over taking your innocence, I cannot stop thinking of you. The softness of your skin, your silken heat, and your sweet gasps as you received pleasure. I want you again, Chloe, more than I've wanted anyone in a long, long time."

She sucked in a breath at his primitive words. "It isn't wise."

He pulled her into his arms. "You're right. Nothing about us is wise. But tell me that you didn't dream of my touch last night." He slid his hand around her neck, his thumb stroking the underside of her jaw. His lips hovered above hers.

Her skin instantly heated and tingled. She could feel the warmth of his lean body and smell the richly masculine scent of his skin. She did want more, craved it with every cell in her body. Yet she was highly conscious they were in the hall of the orphanage. Mrs. Porter or Mr. Whitleson could come upon them at any time. "I did dream of it," she breathed.

"Then say the word, sweet Chloe. And we'll both have what we crave. I'll protect your privacy. Say yes." His lips grazed her throat, and his tongue traced the wildly throbbing pulse at her neck. Her senses spun, and her breasts strained against the fabric of her chemise. Just knowing he still desired her even after they'd already been together was an aphrodisiac. Each moment that passed, she fell deeper under his spell.

Madness.

She struggled to keep hold of the fragments of her control. She shook her head. "I cannot risk an unwanted child."

"There are ways to prevent an unwanted pregnancy. Trust me."

Trust him.

He'd possessed the wherewithal and control to withdraw from her body when they'd been together. She hadn't even thought of it at the time—she'd been consumed by lust. Neither had he revealed her past to her sisters or their husbands. She would most certainly have heard from her family if he had. And as far as she knew, he hadn't whispered a word to the gentlemen at his clubs, or to the patronesses of Almack's, or the influential ladies of the *ton* at their balls. Such scandalous gossip would have reached Huntingdon or her sisters. Never in her wildest dreams did she think she'd trust the Duke of Cameron. But somewhere along the way, she *had* grown to trust him.

She could no longer deny the truth to herself. She wanted this man. Desperately.

But she also wanted the security of a wedding ring.

He lightly nipped her ear, and a shiver of delight coursed down her spine. "Come home with me. Let me pleasure you the way I long to." His voice was raspy with need.

She couldn't risk everything. The path toward complete social ruin was too harsh a reality. She'd never be able to marry a man with a title or money. She'd be left a victim. Just like her father had left her. The thought had the same effect as if a bucket of ice water were dumped over her head.

She pushed against his hard chest. "No. I cannot. You claim that you don't want to marry, but I do. I want more."

He released her and stepped back. "You're right. You deserve more. But it's not something I can offer."

Chapter Fifteen

Michael escorted Chloe outside the orphanage. His crested carriage and matching bays waited along with the hackney she'd hired. He wanted to send the hackney away, carry her into his carriage, and press her back against the cushioned seats and kiss and lick every inch of her satiny skin.

She was right to reject his offer. She deserved to be properly courted with flowers and chocolates and leisurely rides in Hyde Park. She deserved a wedding ring. If only he could offer her those things.

"I can drive you home and drop you off at the corner. No one will see," he said, his voice hoarse to his own ears.

She shook her head. "We both know that being in close quarters is not a good idea."

He nodded. "As you wish."

He'd learned more about her today. She'd taken an ill child under her wing. It was clear she cared deeply for Emily, and he wondered what would happen to Chloe if the child passed away. He knew better than anyone that life could be cruel. He'd give anything to have his best friend back. He'd also happily give up the dukedom to have his brother and father return.

Chloe had learned the harsh lessons of reality early. Her father was a criminal art forger, a man who'd fleeced many members of the *ton*. Like her parent, she'd also been a thief, but Michael was hard-pressed to think of her as a criminal. She hadn't stolen for profit or selfishness or to line her pockets at the expense of others. Rather, she'd carried the burden of guilt, as if her illness was her fault and she was a financial drain on her sisters—a drain she felt the need to remedy by the only means available to her.

He could no longer compare her to her father. He hadn't lied when he'd told her he admired her loyalty to her sisters and her resourcefulness. Yes, she'd picked pockets of those who had more than enough, but what were her choices? London was full of poor and needy. A young woman with Chloe's beauty would have few choices to earn money other than in the many seedy brothels that populated the city streets. The thought of her falling victim to a cruel, flesh peddler made his fists clench at his sides.

Waving away her driver, Michael opened her door and helped her step into the conveyance.

She turned to look at him. "Thank you again for sitting with Emily. I guarantee she will be retelling your story of the dragon and the prince to anyone who will listen."

"It was my pleasure. I look forward to telling her more stories."

Soft pink lips curled in a smile. Leaning forward in her seat, she brushed those lips across his cheek. "Good-bye, Your Grace."

He stiffened. Every nerve ending in his body fired, ready to pounce. To crush her mouth to his in an opened-mouthed kiss. It didn't matter that they were in broad daylight on a city street.

What was it about this woman that made him act irrationally? To want what he knew he could never have?

Tamping down his need, he shut the door and watched as the hackney rattled down the cobbled street. Chloe Somerton may claim that she didn't want him, but he'd seen the rapid pulse at her neck and heard her sharp intake of breath when he'd touched her. She wanted him as much as he wanted her.

He'd thought that once he'd bedded her, he'd have his fill. What a fool he'd been. One taste had only served to heighten his craving. He understood her objections. She wanted to marry, and he could never claim a wife. He clenched his fists at his side. If only he'd returned from the war in complete control of his demons, if only Lord Sefton hadn't died, if only…

There were too many regrets, and nothing would come of it. Marriage was not for damaged soldiers, no matter that he'd returned to claim a dukedom.

He turned away but didn't go to his carriage. Instead, he found himself retracing his steps into the orphanage. What he'd seen earlier had opened his eyes and sparked a different type of interest.

As soon as he entered the vestibule, a tall, thin man with a head of graying black hair approached. "Welcome, Your Grace. I am Mr. Whitleson and I oversee the orphanage. Forgive me for not welcoming you earlier. I was outside with the children and wasn't aware of your presence. As a military man, I'm sure you understand the importance of a schedule."

"For soldiers, yes. Children require a bit more flexibility," Michael said.

"Yes, of course," Whitleson quickly agreed. "Please come into my office, where we can share a drink and you can tell me of your business."

Michael followed the man into a small room crammed with bookshelves and books. Stacks of papers with stone paperweights covered the surface of an oak desk. Whitleson opened a desk drawer and removed a bottle of brandy and two glasses. He poured a good amount into each glass and handed Michael a drink before taking a chair across from him. "Now, please tell me how I may be of assistance."

Michael sipped his drink. "There is a child here who interests me."

Whitleson's eyes widened. "May I ask which one?"

Michael had expected Whitleson's initial surprise. He knew the idea of a duke interested in an orphan would be a rare occurrence. "Her name is Emily. I do not know her last name."

"Emily Higgins? The child has been garnering interest of late." Whitleson's gaze sharpened. "A lady visits young Emily quite often. Perhaps you know her. Miss Chloe Somerton?"

Michael felt a moment of unease. Whitleson was definitely curious and fishing for information. He must know that Michael had visited Emily alongside Chloe. The staff would have informed him. Michael decided it was best to be truthful. Any denial would arouse the man's suspicions further. "I know of her interest in the child," Michael said.

A knowing look crossed Whitleson's face. "Yes. Miss Somerton has grown quite attached to Emily. I'm afraid to be the bearer of bad news, but the child is quite ill."

"I'm aware of her condition. I'm also aware that the visiting doctor is treating her at the orphanage. I would like to send my own physician to examine the child."

"I'm afraid that would be for naught. Nothing else can be done for—"

"I'd also like to make a monetary contribution of clothing and shoes for all the children."

"That's very generous, Your Grace."

"Would five thousand pounds suffice?"

Whitleson choked on his drink, his Adam's apple bobbing

before he swallowed and cleared his throat. "The children will be well cared for with such a generous donation."

"Good. I shall send my physician, Dr. Graves, today to see to Emily."

Whitleson nodded. "Yes. Yes, of course."

"One more thing. I'd like my contributions and my physician's treatment to be kept in the strictest confidence. No one must know. Including Miss Somerton. Understand?"

Mr. Whitleson frowned. No doubt it was an unusual request. Wealthy benefactors wished their names to be known. Donations were rarely made out of selflessness.

"It shall be as you wish."

• • •

A knock sounded on the front door as Chloe descended the grand staircase on her way to the dining room for the evening meal. Rather than wait for the butler, she opened it herself.

"Amelia!" Chloe cried out, thrilled to see her middle sister and her husband, Lord Vale, on the front step.

"Hello, Chloe," Lord Vale said with a charming smile as he guided his wife inside.

"Chloe, dear. I've missed you." Amelia's smile was alive with affection and delight as she hugged Chloe.

Marriage agreed with her sister. Amelia had always been stunning, with auburn hair and blue eyes, but her complexion now glowed with happiness.

"Please tell me you've returned to town for the remainder of the Season," Chloe said.

"Yes. Rosehill may be lovely in the summer, but I'm happy to return." Rosehill was the Vales' country seat in Hampshire, and all three sisters had spent a lovely two weeks in the country for a house party to celebrate Lord Vale's sister's betrothal last summer.

"I admit to not wanting to share my wife, but Amelia did miss you and Eliza terribly," Vale said, placing a possessive arm around Amelia's shoulders.

A stab of jealousy pierced Chloe's chest. Would she ever have a man who loved and cherished her? A man who would move heaven and earth to be with her? Someone who accepted her for her flaws, including *all* her past sins?

Both her sisters had found happiness with their spouses. Chloe didn't think she'd be as fortunate.

"Where's Huntingdon?" Vale asked. "I'd like to catch up."

"He's in his study," Chloe said.

The butler finally appeared to take Lord and Lady Vale's belongings, and Vale disappeared down the hall to find Huntingdon.

A shriek above the stairs captured the sisters' attention, and they looked above to see Eliza fly down the stairs. "At last! I thought you would miss my dinner party."

Chloe's stomach tightened at the mention of Eliza's upcoming party. She hadn't had a moment alone with Eliza since her sister had invited Henry to Huntingdon house yesterday. Eliza had been out of the house, making social calls or with her husband. The one time they'd been together was at the dressmakers, and Madame Adalene had stayed in the fitting room for their entire visit. As a result, Eliza had no idea of Chloe's dilemma and that she was no longer interested in Henry.

"What dinner party?" Amelia said.

"I'm hosting a small gathering Friday evening. Our youngest sister," Eliza said, glancing at Chloe with a mischievous smile, "has captured the interest of an earl."

"Oooh, you must tell all." Amelia looked to Chloe.

Chloe's thoughts were jagged and painful, and a heaviness centered in her chest. How could she tell her sisters she no longer desired Henry because she was fast becoming obsessed with the duke instead? She should gather her courage and speak, but something held her back and the words wouldn't come. Would Huntingdon and Vale force the duke to the altar if her sisters told their husbands the truth?

Good grief. That wouldn't do at all. She wanted a husband, but not a forced one.

"I'll tell you everything over tea," Eliza said. "You must be parched. I'd be a bad hostess if I didn't offer you refreshment after your long journey."

Minutes later, they were all seated in the parlor. A maid wheeled in a tea tray and a plate of scones. Eliza poured the tea and handed Amelia and Chloe steaming cups.

"Now which earl has Chloe captivated?" Amelia said.

"Eliza is speaking of Lord Sefton," Chloe said.

Eliza sat on the edge of her seat. "He's young and quite handsome with fair hair. He's also recently come into the title after his father was tragically killed at Waterloo."

Amelia lowered her teacup and looked at Chloe. "I'm sorry to hear about the death of the father, but I'm happy for you, Chloe. I know you've always wanted to marry a titled gentleman."

Chloe inwardly cringed at her sister's words. She knew her sister didn't mean for her to sound like a fortune-seeking female, but nevertheless, the statement made her feel shallow. But that's what she'd always wanted, wasn't it? A wealthy, titled man. A man who wanted a beautiful, dutiful wife who would seamlessly slip into the role of his countess and run his home and charm his guests.

She'd always justified her goals and believed she was different from the desperate debutantes and their calculating mamas. She didn't care a whit about acceptance by the *ton* or acquiring tickets to the hallowed halls of Almack's. Her motivations had to do with a fear of poverty, abandonment, and sickness.

"The Earl of Sefton is quite smitten," Eliza said. "It's a pleasure to watch him fawn over Chloe. The only obstacle has been the Duke of Cameron."

"The duke?" Amelia looked at Eliza in confusion. "Vale has spoken of the duke. He's a war hero, a former lieutenant colonel, who returned from battle only to discover his father and brother had been killed in an unfortunate accident. What does he have to do with Chloe's earl?"

"The duke owes Henry's father his life," Chloe said softly. "The former Lord Sefton took a bullet in the chest to save him. The duke now thinks of himself as Henry's protector of sorts, even though Henry is a grown man himself."

"Hmm," Amelia said. "And the duke doesn't find you good enough for Henry? I can only assume it is because of our infamous father." Amelia's tone was cutting. Out of all three of the sisters, Amelia had the least regard for their father. Chloe always thought it was because Amelia was the only one to inherit his artistic ability to forge priceless works of art. It was a talent Amelia had resented for years.

Amelia's marriage to Lord Vale had been a saving grace. Rather than forbid her from picking up a brush, her husband encouraged her artistic ambitions to paint images of the laboring poor of London, a calling that had appealed to Amelia ever since their brief time in St. Giles.

"It no longer matters. We have both married earls who are not bothered by Jonathan Miller's crimes. Even Huntingdon, as an art critic who'd been duped by Father, no longer cares," Eliza said.

Chloe didn't want to admit the truth. Michael wasn't overly concerned about their father's corruption, either. He'd been initially more concerned about *her* sins. But now that she'd told him she was no longer interested in Henry, she didn't believe Michael cared much about her past. A deeply buried part of her wanted to confess everything to her sisters, but she had kept the truth to herself for so long she couldn't find the courage to blurt it out now. Where would she even start?

I picked pockets and sold goods to an infamous brothel owner so that I could help pay for my medicine.

Then there was her most recent transgression. *I also lost my virginity and spent an earth-shattering afternoon in the Duke of Cameron's bed.*

She wasn't certain which would be more shocking.

"I've thought of a perfect distraction for the duke and have invited Lady Willowby to join us again Friday evening. My tactic worked when we all attended Vauxhall Gardens."

Chloe's heart sank. Lady Willowby would come? She would have to watch the attractive lady flirt with Michael. How could she get through the evening?

Amelia was watching her closely. "You don't seem excited, Chloe. In fact, you look rather…melancholy." Chloe squirmed beneath Amelia's gaze. As the artist, Amelia was by far the most perceptive.

"I know what it is," Eliza said.

Chloe looked at Eliza in surprise.

Eliza gave her a look of sympathy mingled with worry. "Chloe's been having nightmares again."

Nightmares? Chloe stared wordlessly at her sisters, her heart pounding. "How do you know?"

Eliza patted her hand. "I've heard you at night."

"I thought it had been years," Amelia said. "Perhaps a physician can help."

Summoning the physician was the last thing Chloe wanted. He'd order a tincture of laudanum, and Chloe hated the lethargic effects of the drug.

"No. A physician isn't necessary. I've been sleeping better. I also have a good feeling that after your gathering, things will improve."

"Are you certain?" Eliza asked.

"Without a doubt. Please don't worry."

Everything would be settled Friday evening. She'd patiently explain to Henry that they weren't well suited. He'd understand and would turn his efforts elsewhere. As for Michael, she'd be careful to never be alone with him again, and this madness between them would end once and for all.

All would be well. It had to be.

Chapter Sixteen

Chloe made her way to the kitchens, where she spotted the cook, Mary, taking a tray of scones out of the oven and setting them on a rack to cool.

"Good afternoon," Chloe said.

Mary straightened at the sight of Chloe standing in the doorway. "Is there anything you need, Miss Chloe?" Although Mary was only a few years older than Chloe, the crow's-feet around her eyes and her graying hair made her appear a decade older.

"May I have a word in private?" Chloe asked.

A moment of unease flashed across Mary's face and she wiped her hands on her apron. "If this is about last night's meal, I apologize about the goose. I know it's a greasy bird, but—"

"The meal was delicious. I want to ask your husband a few questions."

"My husband?"

"Yes, about the war." Chloe recalled Alice telling her that the cook's husband had difficulties after the war, and the information had drawn her to the kitchens today.

Mary's face fell. "I don't know. Ben hasn't been himself since his return."

"I understand your hesitation, but I have an...an acquaintance. He's suffered since his return from war as well. I was hoping Ben could help."

After Chloe had seen Michael at the orphanage, she had been determined to cease thinking of him. Yet here she was asking if there were other soldiers who suffered similar symptoms and if the duke could be helped. The thought that there was someone out there who could possibly aid Michael was a draw she couldn't resist.

Mary took a deep breath, then nodded. "Wait here, miss."

Minutes later, Ben entered the room. A tall, thin man with blond hair and bushy sideburns, he had difficulty meeting Chloe's gaze.

"Thank you for speaking with me," Chloe said.

Ben shuffled his feet on the floor. "My wife said you had an acquaintance who suffers from war sickness."

"I do. He has nightmares. Difficulty sleeping. But the most troublesome are the episodes or fits that come on unexpectedly. Anything can trigger them. Loud noises such as fireworks. The sight of Napoleon's carriage at a museum."

Ben lifted his head and met her eyes. There was a deep-seated anguish in the brown depths of his gaze.

Chloe struggled to stay calm and not raise her voice. "Is there anything that can help? Anyone? A particular army physician who has had success treating these symptoms?"

Mary scoffed. "The army doctors wanted to cut and bleed him. They are useless."

"Not all soldiers experience symptoms upon their return. The physicians believe only weak soldiers are so afflicted," Ben spoke up.

The weak ones? Of all the names she'd called the Duke

of Cameron since she'd met him, weak was not one of them. He'd been an officer in charge of countless lives, and she'd heard stories of his capable command during the chaos of war.

For the first time, she understood why he hadn't sought aid from the army. If they thought him weak and inferior and wanted to bleed him, why would he?

Chloe was enraged. Bloodletting wouldn't help. It wasn't a physical illness but one of the mind.

"It wasn't until we talked with other soldiers that the symptoms eased," Mary said.

"Please tell me," Chloe implored.

"You must talk about your fears, even the worst of those," Ben said.

"I'm not sure he will cooperate. My acquaintance blames himself for things he could not have changed. Decisions that were made for him."

Ben sighed. "No solider wants to relive their most fearful memories of battle. I avoided it like the plague, but it did little to aid me and only served to make the nightmares worse. Your friend must face his fears, and the only way to do that is by talking about them. It may be difficult to speak about the worst days of your life, but it becomes easier over time. I was fortunate to have Mary and a fellow solider to talk to."

"What happened to your other comrades who suffered from war sickness?" Chloe asked.

Ben shook his head regretfully. "They were not so fortunate, miss. The army sent two to the asylum. Both hung themselves within three months."

Lord. It was just as her maid Alice had told her. The army must ship them off to asylums to die rather than attempt to heal its own soldiers. "I'm sorry."

The thought of that happening to Michael made Chloe feel nauseated. Could she help him when she swore to stay away from him?

She could write him a letter explaining what she'd learned from Ben. She prayed he would take the advice or at least seek out other soldiers with similar conditions so that he wasn't alone. But just as the thought occurred to her, she pushed it aside. In her heart, she knew it wouldn't work. The duke was too proud to take written advice or to seek out other soldiers with similar conditions on his own. She'd have to visit him and convince him herself.

Could she do it? Could she go to his home, knowing the attraction between them was as strong as lightning. Could she resist him?

It was a risk. But she'd seen him suffer not once, but twice, and she felt a strong need to aid him.

She'd have to be careful sneaking out of Huntingdon's house. She'd tell Michael what she'd learned, urge him to take the first steps to recovery, while maintaining a firm resolve to keep a physical distance between them. It was the best she could do. Anything else and it would be more than her reputation in jeopardy.

It would be her heart.

Chapter Seventeen

Chloe woke feeling more uncertain than ever. She'd spent the night tossing and turning in bed as sleep evaded her. She'd dreamed of Michael's kiss, his strong hands caressing the soft skin of her thigh…the glorious feel of him pressed against her.

She'd finally fallen asleep only to wake at dawn in a sweat. Heart pounding, she kicked aside her twisted sheets and sat on the edge of her bed. Despite the risks, she'd made up her mind to try to help the Duke of Cameron.

Chloe slipped out of bed, stuffed her feet in slippers, and summoned her maid. She dressed quickly in a demure blue gown with embroidered rosettes at the bodice and hem. It was Thursday, her day to visit the orphanage, but for the first time she felt a pressing need to visit another destination first. A short carriage ride later, she arrived at the Berkeley Square mansion.

Her knock was answered quickly. Surprisingly, the duke's butler, Hodges, did not look down on her with haughty disdain when he opened the door to find her on the doorstep.

"Good day, miss," he said as he held the door open for

her.

She marveled at the butler's change in demeanor. He was quite hospitable and treated her with respect, but when she handed him her cloak, something about his expression gave her pause. He opened his mouth, then shut it, as if unsure what to say, when the housekeeper, Mrs. Smith, walked into the vestibule, followed by an older gentleman with bushy eyebrows and a slightly protruding brow. He was carrying a black bag.

"Miss Somerton! It's good to see you." Mrs. Smith turned to the man by her side. "This is Dr. Graves, the duke's physician. Doctor, this is Miss Somerton."

Apprehension made the hair on Chloe's nape rise. Was someone in the household ill? Was it Michael?

Dr. Graves acknowledged Chloe with a brief nod. "It's a pleasure to make your acquaintance, Miss Somerton. Please excuse me, as I have another appointment this morning." Hodges offered his hat and cane, and the physician departed.

"It's good you're here," Mrs. Smith said.

The knot in Chloe's stomach tightened. Something *was* amiss. "Is the duke well?"

Mrs. Smith lowered her voice. "He's had another fit. We summoned Dr. Graves straightway. He left a sedative, but the duke refuses to take it."

Chloe stepped toward the winding staircase that led to the second floor.

"He's not in his bedchamber, miss," the housekeeper said. "He's in his study, and he refuses to leave and barks at anyone who tries to enter." She wrung her hands. "He's a good man, but he threatened to sack any member of the staff who disturbs him, and we're fearful of him when he has these tirades. It's almost as if he still thinks he's fighting the war."

Chloe wasn't entirely certain what the housekeeper meant. How could the duke's staff believe he thought he'd returned to war? Had he donned his uniform, loaded his pistols? Was he marching back and forth across the room?

"I'll see to him," Chloe said.

Hodges stepped forward, but Chloe raised a hand. "I know the way, and it's best if I'm alone." She hurried down the hall. She knew exactly where the study was, since it was where she first met Michael when she'd visited his home weeks ago.

She reached the door and rapped on the wood. No response. She rapped again, louder this time. When there still was no reply, she opened the door and swept inside, bracing herself for the worst.

She halted midstep.

Sweet Lord. The room was ransacked. Unrolled maps of varying sizes lay on every inch of the Oriental carpet. Books were scattered across the floor in what appeared to be a haphazard pattern. Some were open, others closed. A large globe was removed from its stand and rested on the floor in the corner. Glasses from the sideboard littered the floor as well. At first she thought the books had been carelessly tossed onto the carpet from the bookshelves, but she realized they were strategically placed on the curled edges of the maps to prevent them from rolling. The globe and the glasses were also used to keep the papers flat. The longest map was splayed across the large mahogany desk.

Michael stood behind the desk, palms flat on the surface as he studied the map like a general before a major battle. He was dressed in shirtsleeves—his cravat, jacket, and waistcoat strewn across a chair. He looked up at her intrusion, his sharp, dark eyes assessing her in a way that made her nerves flutter in her stomach.

"Your butler told me I could find you here. Please don't blame the man for not announcing me," she said.

His mouth twisted wryly. "Ah, it seems you have charmed my staff. Why am I not surprised?"

"They are concerned," she replied.

His eyes flashed in a familiar display of impatience. "Are they? Can't a man seek some peace in his own home?"

"Quiet is one thing. Hours alone and threatening to dismiss your servants when they are genuinely worried for you is another thing entirely. They summoned Dr. Graves. He left a sedative."

"I don't need a damned sedative," he said in a harsh, raw voice.

"They believe you are reliving the war," she said softly. "Has something triggered another episode?" She feared he would force her to leave, but he raised his hand and pointed to the map before him.

"See for yourself."

Every inch of him looked hard and merciless. Gathering her courage, she approached and looked down at the map spread across the massive desk. Light and dark pencil markings were drawn across the map along with hand-written notes in small, neat print. She leaned closer and read the names of two villages south of Brussels. "What is this?"

"It shows the battle plans that day," he said.

She suspected the answer, but she asked anyway. "Which day?"

"Waterloo."

She glanced up at his face, unsure if he was having an episode or not. She could see the day's growth of stubble on his chin and cheekbones. His hair was ruffled like he'd repeatedly run his fingers through it in agitation. His shirt clung to his broad shoulders and the top two buttons were undone, revealing the muscles of his throat and a mat of crisp hair on his chest. Memories returned in a rush—the heat of his body coursing down the entire length of hers, her breasts crushed against the hardness of his chest, his tongue exploring the peaks of her breasts.

She looked at his wrinkled brow and tried to swallow the lump in her throat. How could this strong, virile man be tortured?

She pointed to some of the handwritten notes. "What do these mean?"

He sighed. "They are battle strategies I could have used to save Lord Sefton, Henry's father. If only my men had been positioned here"—he pointed to a spot on the map below a large hill—"instead of here"—he pointed to another location close to a road—"Lord Sefton would still be alive."

Her heart pounded as she looked at him. He *was* having an episode of sorts.

Guilt. He was suffering from overwhelming guilt for surviving a war when he believed he should have been killed instead of his friend.

She recognized the crippling emotion. She'd suffered from it all her life. Guilt for being sick. Guilt for not being able to help her sisters when they'd been abandoned, homeless, and hungry. Guilt for suffering from a lingering illness that prevented her from aiding with an equal share of the work at the print shop.

She studied his chiseled profile. "You cannot change the past, but you must look to the future. I know this more than anyone."

He took a deep breath, his fingers curling around the edges of the desk. Although he wasn't as bad off as when she'd awakened him from his nightmare, he was clearly suffering. In an instant, all the anxiety she'd felt about visiting him and aiding him vanished.

She watched him bent over his desk, his jaw clenched in torment, and her heart ached. Only a good man with a strong conscience would be staring at an old war map, trying to figure out how he could have saved his best friend's life. How long would he suffer for his friend's decision to sacrifice himself?

Years? A decade? Forever?

For the first time, she truly understood his dedication to protect Henry from harm.

Before she could stop herself, she touched his cheek. His skin was warm, and the scrape of whiskers on her palm sent a shiver down her spine.

He stiffened, but did not pull away from her touch. Rather, he placed a hand over hers and cradled it against his cheek. "I'm not having a full episode, not like during the fireworks. But the truth is that I live in fear of another trigger. At times, the unpredictability frightens me more than the actual event."

The anguish and honesty behind his words touched a deep part of her soul. She fought hard against the tears she refused to let fall. He needed strength and faith. "You must learn to accept the past and live for the future. You are now a *duke.*"

He laughed bitterly. "I know my ducal responsibilities. But how can I marry and have children when I live day to day, not knowing what or when something will cause me to react irrationally? I'm a volcano on the verge of erupting. Christ, what if I turn violent? How could I take such a risk? How could I condemn another to such a fate?"

"I don't believe that." She'd never feared physical harm from him. She feared losing her heart instead.

She may not be able to change his mind, but she may be able to help him. She took a step closer. Warmth radiated from his tightly coiled body. "I spoke with someone who had similar experiences as you. There is a treatment. It's not a cure, but it may ease your symptoms."

He veered back to look at her, his eyes sharp and assessing. "You talked to a soldier? About me?"

She met his gaze. "There's no need to get upset. I never mentioned your name."

"It's not that. It's just that no one has ever thought to do that for me. Not my staff, not Dr. Graves, not Henry. If I didn't know any better, I'd say you care, Chloe Somerton."

She held her breath. How much to admit? She'd never lied to herself in the past and she wouldn't start now. If this were going to work, there had to be truthfulness between them. "Yes. I do care. You are not alone."

He reached for her hand, turned it palm up, and placed a warm kiss to the center. Breathing lightly between parted lips, she trembled from the contact.

He lifted his head and looked into her eyes. "I was wrong about you from the very beginning. You are no charlatan, Chloe. You are the most honest woman I know."

Honest.

She had never been completely honest with anyone. Not her sisters. Not him.

At a point when he should be emotionally exposed, she found that she was the most vulnerable. A frightening realization washed over her. She was in love with him. Deeply in love. From the beginning, she'd been drawn to him. She loved his height, his strength, and his masculinity. She loved his intelligence and his loyalty to his deceased best friend. She even admired his strong moral code to look after Henry.

She could turn and run and ponder her frightening feelings or she could stay and attempt to help him. She watched him lift his arm and brush his fingers against her cheek. The tenderness of his touch made her decision easy.

She took a breath. "I think you should try something."

He lowered his hand. "I cannot. I've heard of others and what the army does to them. Straps. Bloodletting. Asylums with horrible, filthy conditions that drive men to hang themselves from the rafters. In essence, torture. I know as a duke I wouldn't be sent to an asylum and treated the same, but they would mark me as mad. The physicians would descend upon the house with their bloodletting knives or jars of leeches and tinctures of laudanum."

She swallowed hard. "No. That's not what I meant. The solider I spoke with is the husband of Huntingdon's cook. He did not go to the army for treatment but used a different method and had a measure of success."

"How?"

"You must face your greatest fear."

He turned away. "The battle is long over."

"You misunderstand. You must talk about that day. Relive it. All of it."

"To whom?"

She propped a hip on the desk and faced him. "To me. Talk to me. Tell me everything," she implored.

A look of discomfort crossed his face. "I don't know if I'm able. It's my weakness, my curse to bear."

"I don't see it that way. There's nothing to be ashamed of. You are a man who experienced tragedy and who feels a great amount of guilt for things you couldn't control. I don't see you as weak at all. I see you as *human.*"

"Chloe, I don't want to disappoint you."

Reaching up, she cradled his face until he saw the determination in her eyes. "It's safe. I won't repeat a word you utter in this room. Trust me."

Chapter Eighteen

Trust me. Michael had uttered the same words to Chloe not long ago. Was he able to do what she asked? Was he able to relive that day? He'd shut out the past for so many different reasons. The triggers, when they occurred, were bad enough. His mind would travel without his will until he was a sweating, quivering, mass of nerves. He hated the weakness. The nauseating sickness. Could he intentionally bring it on, let alone in front of her?

"Go on," she urged.

He hesitated. If there were any chance this could help, shouldn't he try? He took a breath, held it in, let it out slowly as he counted to ten. "It rained all the night before and well into the morning. As a result, the ground was sodden. Napoleon had decided to hold off on his attack because he was worried about moving his artillery and men. It was a decision that led to his defeat."

The horrible weather conditions and the events of the battle had been reported in the papers for months after the war. Stories about how Napoleon's hesitation had aided the

Anglo-led allied army, under the command of the Duke of Wellington, by allowing the Prussian army to arrive in time were well known.

"My men were stationed by the road here," he said, pointing to a row of small Xs on the map. "I was to keep them there until I received orders. Sefton was in my regiment and my second-in-command. It was damp and humid. Our officers' coats were wool, and our rain-sodden uniforms added ten pounds of weight. Sweat rolled down our brows, our backs, and into our eyes. We waited in the morning mist for hours until the battle began."

His hands started to shake, and he fisted them on the desk. Chloe began to rub his back with long smooth strokes of her slender fingers. He forced himself to keep breathing, in then out, and focus on her beside him—a lock of blond hair that had escaped her pins and curled around the shell of her ear, the porcelain smoothness of her cheek, the parting of her pink lips, the dark blue chips in her irises.

"When we finally started to charge, the clash of the battle was horrific—like nothing I'd ever heard before. Men cried out as they were shot or bayoneted, horses fell screaming, and the cannon fire…Christ…it was deafening."

She stepped closer and kept stroking his back in calming motions. She touched his hand and his fingers curled around hers. The words came easier now, faster. "We were defeating the enemy forces, but not without suffering bad causalities. I quickly lost count of the number of men under my command who fell, as well as the bodies of enemy soldiers who littered the battlefield. The already damp earth grew slippery from mud and blood. What seemed like hours later, the battle slowed. I was exhausted, parched, and drenched in sweat when I saw him out of the corner of my eye."

"Lord Sefton?"

"No, a French soldier. His pistol was raised and he was

charging from behind. I reached for a knife in my boot, but in that instant, I knew I'd never withdraw the blade and throw it in time." His eyes closed as the vivid image returned, hard and unmerciful. "I remember his face, pockmarked, a cheek smeared with blood, blond hair plastered to his scalp with sweat and grime. Sefton saw the solider and launched himself at me. I hit the ground hard just as a pistol exploded and struck Sefton in the chest." Michael's fingers tightened around hers, holding on like a lifeline.

"And then?" Her voice was low but steady.

"I didn't stop to help my friend—my rage was so great. I went after the enemy, ran him down, ignored his pleas, and slit his throat. Not only did Sefton take a bullet for me, but I didn't stop to comfort him and hold his hand while he took his last breath. I wasn't there for him, dammit, after what he'd done for me."

He gritted his teeth and tightened his shoulders. He felt a rising panic, but by sheer force of will kept it at bay.

"Look at me, Michael. Keep going," she said.

He could do this. He *would* do this. "I went back and sat beside Sefton. Held him until a soldier under my command shook me and told me that I had to let my friend go. That was when I reached inside his blood-soaked officer's coat and found his letter."

"He asked you to look after Henry," she said.

"Yes. He needn't have written it. I knew his wishes long before."

Never before had he spoken about that day to anyone. He had sliced open his wounds, and although he felt shaken, the usual triggers had not sent him into a dark panic. He was in control of his mind *and* body. He looked in her eyes, bottomless depths of blue that a man could easily drown. He could stare into them forever.

Forever.

What a traitorous thought. He could never have that, could he? No, forever was not for men like him. Preparing himself for the inevitable disappointment, his eyes met hers. "You know it all."

She hesitated, her beautiful eyes watching him. "I think you are the bravest, most honorable man I know."

He sucked in a breath as her words sunk in. She didn't look at him with pity or disgust. She didn't step back or glance away.

But just because he was able to speak of the past without going into a dark void didn't mean he was cured. "Chloe, I don't know what you expected, but this doesn't mean I'm cure —"

"*Shhh.*" She pressed a finger against his lips. "You did nothing wrong. Your friend knew what he was doing when he chose to step in front of that soldier. He chose to save you. Altering the battle plans that day may or may not have changed the outcome, but it was *not* your fault."

The armor that guarded his chest cracked. The honesty he saw in the sapphire depths of her eyes slowly chipped away at the burden of guilt he'd carried for so long. Along with the relief came a desire to claim her so strong that his hands shook. She must have read it. Her eyes flared, and she licked her lips.

His mouth swooped down to capture hers. Miraculously, she didn't push him away but clung to him. He kissed her without finesse, but with a raw primal need. Her soft moans fueled his lust, and he thrust his tongue inside her honeyed mouth and explored her like a man starved. He was parched, wandering alone in a desert, and she was his oasis. His hands were everywhere, sliding over silk and skin. He cradled her head and his fingers sank into the luxurious blond tresses.

Hair pins dropped to the desk and her hair fell about her shoulders. He buried his face in the golden glory and breathed in her unique scent of lemongrass. "I love your hair, your scent."

She moaned, and he returned to her mouth and placed lingering kisses on the corners of her lips. "I've never known anyone like you. Special. Rare. Sweet." He nuzzled her ear. "I burn for you."

She sighed, a lovely sound. "I burn for you, too."

"God, to be inside you once more."

"Yes," she breathed. "Once more."

His heart jolted in his chest. "I want to see you. All of you without a stitch of clothing."

Blue eyes widened. "It's the middle of the afternoon. Your staff."

"They wouldn't dare enter."

She nodded. His fingers deftly unbuttoned her gown and pushed back the silk. She slipped her arms through the sleeves, and the fabric slid down her body to pool at her feet. She stepped out of the fabric, and he unfastened her petticoat, and it followed the path of the gown. Large hands grasped her hips and spun her around to untie her stays. She turned to stand before him clad only in her shift and silk stockings, and was more enticing to him than any woman he'd ever laid eyes upon.

"Will you remove your shift?"

She swallowed, clearly nervous. But she was his Chloe, brave and daring. When her hands went to the straps of the thin garment, he thought he would burst with need. Slowly she raised the hem over her head and dropped it to the floor.

His eyes feasted on her creamy flesh. Her skin was soft, her breasts lush and full, her waist narrow, and her legs long and slim. "You're so beautiful."

He picked her up and sat her on the desk. The map crinkled beneath her, and he didn't care. His thoughts were focused solely on her. On her slightly parted lips, the rise and fall of her chest, and the way her pupils slightly expanded when she grew aroused.

God, he wanted this woman.

Stepping closer, he nudged her legs apart with his thighs. He rolled down her stockings until her shapely legs were revealed to his hungry gaze. They were perfect, long and slightly muscled; he envisioned them wrapped around him as he thrust inside her hot, welcoming body.

Easy. She was a gift, and he needed to make this last, needed the memories for the long, sleepless nights ahead.

His hands skimmed her bare legs. "I've lain awake dreaming of kissing and licking you everywhere."

"Everywhere?" she asked, her eyes focused on his face. Her pulse fluttered wildly at her neck.

"Here." Lowering his head, his lips grazed hers. "And here," he said, kissing a hot trail down the column of her slender throat. He lingered where her neck met her shoulder. "And your lovely breasts." He heard her sharp intake of breath as he plumped one lush breast, licked and sucked her hardened nipple, then moved to the other. Her whimpers of pleasure urged him on, and a desire to taste her was so strong his knees nearly buckled. Laying her back on the desk, he greedily nipped and tasted, then his tongue dipped in her navel in a sensual swirl.

"And lower." His palm cupped her sex and she gasped. He lowered to his knees and parted her silky thighs. Her womanly musk that spoke of her arousal made him grow even harder. Christ. If he didn't taste her soon, he'd go mad. He lowered his head, blew gently on the blond curls.

She squirmed, her fingers grasping fistfuls his hair. "Michael?"

"Let me pleasure you." He pressed a kiss to the top of the curls, then gently parted the delicate pink lips of her sex. Then she was bared before him, swollen and wet. Glistening in her feminine glory of arousal. For him. There was something feverishly arousing seeing her spread before him on his desk where he'd spent hours with his maps and his solitude and his memories of war. She was his fantasy, and he never need experience dread or fear or loneliness in this room again. His gaze greedily memorized every inch of her, and the stunningly erotic image burned in his mind and replaced all the others he wanted to forget.

He slid his hands beneath her bottom and raised her to him. With the tip of his tongue, he traced her swollen lips. "Michael!" she cried out.

He ran a finger down the wet slit and she shuddered. The scent of her arousal filled his senses and fueled his arousal. His tongue replaced his finger and the taste of her was like nothing he'd ever experienced. It filled his senses and drove him to the brink. He licked and laved and teased, and when she raised her hips, he gloried in her response.

Her soft moans drove him onward, and when his tongue traced the sensitive pearl at the crest of her sex, she arched high off the desk and into his mouth.

"Oh, my," she whispered. "I never imagined."

He raised his head to meet her gaze. "Let yourself go, love. Come for me."

Her hands threaded in his hair, but this time, she held him against her. He tasted her wet heat as she surrendered completely to his strokes. He loved her soft moans, her uninhibited reaction. He wanted to hear her cry out his name as she found her release. He flicked his tongue where she craved it most, the tiny bud between her thighs that made her tremble and moan. He gave her no quarter, but reveled in the way she shivered and squirmed and gasped.

When her body grew taut in need of release, he slipped a finger inside her tight sheath and swirled his tongue over the sensitive nerves. She cried out, and he felt the tiny tremors of her climax on his finger. He was harder than he'd ever been, aching and heavy, desperate to free his cock and thrust himself deep inside her tightness.

But this was for her, for the singular woman she was. And for what she'd done for him. His heart squeezed with an emotion he dared not name. He may not be able to keep her...to hold onto her forever, but he'd have this memory.

Standing, he held her, kissed her forehead, her eyes, her lips. "To my dying day, I'll never forget how lovely you are in your passion."

Chapter Nineteen

Chloe had never imagined a man could make love to a woman the way Michael had pleasured her. It was glorious, marvelous. She should be ashamed to be naked in the middle of the day sprawled on a duke's desk in his study. She should be ashamed, but shame was the last emotion she felt. What she'd shared with him wasn't just physical, but something intense and emotional. Something rare and special.

Her heart swelled with love.

She raised herself on her elbows. "I'm afraid your map is ruined."

"I hardly care. Are you blushing, Miss Somerton?"

"It is daylight, and I'm lying on your desk without a stitch of clothing. While you are completely dressed, down to your hessians," she pointed out.

He grinned. "A fact that can be quickly remedied."

"Devil," she said, giving him a wicked smile. "The truth is I'm wildly curious about your body."

His expression grew serious. "Chloe, I want you very much, but this was for you."

He meant only to pleasure her. An odd twinge of disappointment pierced her chest. She was curious about his body, and this would be her last chance to explore him. The thought was dismaying, so she forced herself to push it aside. He had shown her unimaginable pleasure, and she wanted to give and receive, to explore and satisfy a burning curiosity, and to make this moment last as long as she could.

"But I long to see you," she said.

"That's dangerous."

"It's good then that I'm not a lady who's easily frightened."

His half-lidded gaze spoke of desire. He wanted her, but he still held back. She shimmied off the desk to stand before him and pressed a hand to his chest. His heart pounded beneath the soft fabric of his shirt. She leaned into him and pressed soft kisses to the corners of his lips, light and teasing. It had the intended result.

He swept her high into his arms as his mouth slanted across hers and deepened the kiss. He carried her away from the desk, kicking aside maps and books that littered the floor as they went, then set her on her feet before the fireplace. The plush Oriental carpet felt decadent beneath her bare feet.

Breathless from his kisses, she reached for the buttons on his shirt. "May I?"

The first buttoned loosened. Soon he was aiding her and pulling it over his head to reveal a long, sinewy torso. Her mouth went dry at the sight of his chest, all hard angles and ridges. She rested her hands on his shoulders and placed a lingering kiss on his collarbone, then let her tongue edge out to lick his hot flesh. He growled deep in his throat, and the rumble made her shiver with pleasure.

She kept going, placing kisses on his chest followed by licks. The growl turned into a groan, his fingers buried in her hair. She kissed and laved each of his flat nipples, then her fingers followed the line of hair down his stomach that disappeared into his trousers.

When his hands rose, she pushed them away and raised her eyes to his. "Let me."

His gaze was hot, intense. "You're going to drive me mad."

"Then it's only fair."

Her fingers went to the fall of his trousers, and she worked the buttons. At last his cock sprang free. Long and hard, it took her breath away. "Oh, my," she breathed. "I want to touch you."

He was quick to divest himself of his boots and clothing, and he nearly jumped out of his skin when her fingers touched his shaft. Her eyes rose to his. "Am I hurting you?"

"God no," he hissed.

"Show me."

"Hold me harder. Stroke me. Up and down. Just like that."

She was tentative at first, a soft brush of her fingers on the head of his cock. She loved the texture of him, the hardness of his shaft and the velvety softness of the tip. His voice was hoarse. "I should have known you'd be a quick learner."

She shot him a seductive look. "Is that bad?"

"You have power."

The thought was scintillating. He'd given her unimaginable pleasure with his mouth, and she wondered if she could do the same for him. Would he like it? Would it be as sinfully pleasurable for him as it was for her? Curious about the texture and taste of him, she lost her inhibitions.

She slipped to her knees and kissed his navel, his hip, and then ran the tip of her tongue over the engorged head.

"Chloe," he hissed.

"It's my turn." Emboldened by his response, she licked him again. He tasted unique and delicious, and the ache grew between her legs. He'd shown her how to hold and stroke him, and she used her lips and hands the same way. She started at the tip, then took him as fully as she could in her mouth, and then worked back up the length and swirled her tongue across the head. His response was explosive, clearly showing how much he enjoyed it, and she became bolder. She loved the rush of his breath, his groans, and the way his fingers dug into her hair. And when her fingers grazed the heavy sac beneath his penis, he jerked and gasped.

"Stop, Chloe. I'll spend."

She raised her head to find him watching her. "I need you, Michael. I need to feel you inside me."

He laid her on the soft carpet and joined her. The feel of skin against skin was magnificent. Her breasts tingled against his hair-roughened chest, and she writhed beneath him, eager to touch more of his body. His tongue tantalized the buds that had swollen to their fullest, and her head fell back at the delicious pleasure. Passion rose in her like the hottest fire, clouding her brain.

He entered her with one powerful thrust, and they both cried out. "I love the feel of you. So hot, so ready for me."

Her body melted against his, and the world was filled with him. Soon their bodies were moving in exquisite harmony. The hot, sliding friction roused her to the peak of desire. He reached between their bodies to touch her there, the sweet spot between her legs that made her tremble. Love flowed through her like warm honey, and she soared higher and higher until her world shattered into pure pleasure. He thrust once more, then threw back his head, and at the last moment, he withdrew, and his hot seed arced across her belly. They collapsed against each other, each gasping for breath.

He rolled to the side and tucked her curves against him. "I'm a changed man."

She leaned back to study his face and caught his grin. She reached out to touch the ruffled dark hair that clung to his damp brow. "Because you spoke of the past?" she teased.

He caught her hand and kissed her palm. "No. Because

of *you*."

Her heartbeat throbbed in her ears. She couldn't tear her gaze away from his handsome profile. "I knew you could talk about the war."

He studied her thoughtfully. "Chloe, I admit that I'm relieved I was able to speak about the battle without triggering an episode, but you must know it could happen again."

"I didn't expect you to be cured. The soldier I spoke with only said it improves over time and that he must keep speaking about the trauma until it is no longer shocking. Only then did his symptoms ease. There is hope for you, Michael."

"Hope," he echoed. "It's a wonderful word and I shall try to remember it." Leaning up on an elbow, he looked at her. "You couldn't have known I was in my study poring over old war maps. Why did you come today?"

She bit her lip. "I kept thinking about your distress from the fireworks. If there was a chance I could help, then I had to try."

"I'm grateful." He brushed her forehead with a kiss. "I've treated you badly in the past, and I owe you a service for helping me. I want you to know that I'd never do anything to harm you."

Harm? Time had changed much between them. She knew he would never reveal that she'd been a pickpocket. At least that secret was safe from her family and society. But there were other secrets from her past, secrets that no one knew, not even Michael. She'd always planned and hoped they would stay deeply buried in the recesses of her mind, but for the first time, she wanted to reveal everything. To share her burdens with another.

Was it possible?

The risks were high. After all they'd shared, she did not believe he would speak of her shameful secrets, but there were other forms of harm, those far more painful than she'd ever imagined.

Disappointment. Disgust. Rejection.

He respected her now, but would he after she told him everything?

She could not stop herself from pondering the question: if speaking about the past had helped Michael, would it help her as well? Her soul ached with the need to unburden her own guilt. Was it possible for her to do so?

She reached for his hand. "I believe I should take my own advice. There's something I wish to tell you."

Chapter Twenty

She waited until they were dressed and sitting side by side next to the hearth. His arm was wrapped around her shoulders and gave her strength. "I haven't told you everything about my past. You have been honest about your own, and I'd like to share mine."

"I'm a good listener."

She could barely meet his gaze. "You know I picked pockets. You know why."

She felt him nod. "To help your sisters pay for your medicine."

"Yes." Her voice was barely above a whisper.

He brushed his lips across her temple. "Go on."

She took a deep breath and gathered her courage. "Mr. Allenson at the apothecary didn't want filched handkerchiefs, brass buttons, or ladies' jeweled pins. He wanted money. So I went to the only place I knew I could trade my filched wares for coin. The Seven Sins brothel. The proprietress, Madame Satine, was a sympathetic woman, and she paid me for the trinkets. She gave them to her girls as rewards. My relationship with Madame was a strictly business arrangement. No one ever learned of it. Not my sisters. Not Huntingdon or Vale. No one."

If the truth came out, the scandal would be enormous. Even worse than when their father's art forgeries were discovered. It didn't matter that she'd never worked on her back in the brothel. Respectable females wouldn't be caught near a brothel, let alone inside the establishment, speaking with its proprietress.

And what was her excuse? She'd stolen items and had sought to sell them for coins.

Goodness. Could it be any worse?

She was afraid to look at him. Afraid to meet his gaze and see disappointment, anger, or worse, that he was *disgusted* by her. How could she blame him? She was ashamed of her past, and she never felt worthy to be in his world. Anguish seared her heart, and she bit back tears.

"Chloe."

She shook her head, afraid to look at him.

"Chloe." His slid a thumb beneath her chin and raised her gaze to his. At his heated look, an all too familiar tingling began in her stomach. Her heart squeezed. His look wasn't repulsive, but warm.

"Is that all?"

She blinked in surprise. "Pardon?"

"Is that all of it?"

A knot inside her stomach eased an inch. Could he possibly think there was more?

She nodded. "That's everything."

"You have held this secret inside for all these years?" he asked.

"Yes."

"You were so young. No one of such tender years should have suffered so gravely. You are a survivor, and you did what you had to do to help your sisters and live. I've known soldiers, trained military men, who'd given up on the battlefield rather than fight to survive as you did. What makes you think I would not admire you?"

"Admire me? I'm ashamed of my past."

"There is nothing to be ashamed of, love."

Love. He'd called her his love. Could he mean it? Or was it a slip of his tongue? Her emotions whirled, and her heart beat frantically in her chest.

He raised her hand and pressed his lips against her palm. "Nothing these hands have done is cause for shame. Release your guilt, Chloe Somerton, just as you have told me to release mine."

She drank in the sweetness of his words and the cooling balm to her soul. She pressed her open lips to his, and she moaned as he cupped the back of her head and held her gently. She quivered at the sweet tenderness of his kiss.

"I love you," she said.

She felt him stiffen, and for a heart-stopping moment, she realized she'd spoken the words out loud.

He pulled back and looked into her eyes. "Marry me."

She stared, thinking she'd imagined the words.

"Will you marry me, Chloe Somerton?"

"Michael, I—" She was afraid to breathe, afraid she'd break the spell.

His eyes darkened with emotion. "You've shown me kindness and bravery, and miraculously, you've given me hope. Hope that there is a chance for me to live a normal life. I'm not a fool to let that slip through my fingers. I know I should speak with both Huntingdon and Vale first, but I cannot wait. Please, say yes, and I shall visit the earls straightway."

Oh my. She wasn't imagining things. He wanted her as a wife, his duchess, even after learning the entire truth. She could barely breathe, let alone find the strength to speak.

"Chloe?"

She moved to kneel before him and cradled his face with both of her hands. "Yes. Yes, I'll marry you."

He kissed her sweetly, gently, and she felt the power within his body. A thought occurred to her and she pulled back. "What about Henry? What do we tell him?"

He let out a deep breath. "The truth. He is my responsibility, and I admit that I haven't treated him fairly. My honor dictates that I look after him, not hurt him, and I shall tell him before I speak with the earls."

"No. You are not the only one who feels guilty for treating him unfairly. In my heart, I've known for some time that there could be no future between us. I want to tell him." This was something she needed to do. She may not be able to change the past, but she could do the right thing in the future.

"Chloe, I don't think —"

"Please. Let me speak with him first. My sister's dinner party is tomorrow night, and I shall speak with him then. Promise me you will not see Henry or visit Huntingdon or Vale until I talk with Henry."

At Michael's hesitation, she urged, "Promise!"

His lips thinned, but he nodded. "All right. I promise. Tomorrow night, not a day later."

Chapter Twenty-One

After Chloe departed, Michael went to his bedchamber. For the first time since returning from the war, he felt a bottomless peace and satisfaction. There were no shadows across his heart. Chloe had come to him, had cared for him, and had helped him overcome his greatest fears. She'd put her trust in him and shared her own past, and he was in awe of her bravery.

Then, miraculously, she'd told him she loved him.

He basked in the knowledge. He'd never believed in love. The emotion was foreign to him. Loyalty, honor, and responsibility—these were traits he understood. But he knew he wanted Chloe in his life, and asking her to marry him was something he'd never thought would be possible for a man with his condition.

He had a new purpose. The future no longer seemed a dark, lonely place with visions of bloody battlefields, the acrid scent of gunpowder, or the terrifying cries of dying soldiers. The nightmares may never cease entirely, but with Chloe by his side, he knew the future was no longer to be dreaded and feared.

He needed to speak with Henry and explain everything. He hoped Henry would come to understand, to learn to forgive him for not confessing the truth sooner. He still intended to uphold his promise to Henry's father and help and guide Henry with the earldom and all its responsibilities. Michael owed a blood debt he'd never fully be able to repay. It would be difficult to honor Chloe's request to speak with Henry first, but Michael understood her need. Chloe felt guilty, just as he did.

Michael paced his bedchamber. He was restless. If he couldn't attend to Henry, then he could see another. He opened the door and called for his valet.

• • •

"Mr. Michael! You came back," Emily said.

Michael smiled at the child in bed. It was the late afternoon, and the room was empty except for Emily. The sounds of children playing outside carried through the sole window. "I promised I would, and dukes never break a promise."

Emily leaned up on her elbows and eyed the book under his arm. "Is it another prince and dragon story?"

"It is. I searched my entire home, including the old nursery for the book. Everyone helped."

"Everyone?"

"My entire household staff. I feared the book was gone, but my housekeeper found it tucked away in one of the spare bedrooms."

Emily giggled. "How many bedrooms do you have?"

"Too many."

"Does the book contain a prince and dragon story?"

"It does." He pulled up a chair, sat by her bedside, and opened the book to the desired page. "But in this one, the dragon sets fire to the forest and the prince has to find his way through the smoldering woods to reach the castle where the princess is kept captive."

Her eyes widened. "Does he?"

"I won't spoil it but will have to read it. But I must warn you that it is a long story."

Animation briefly left her face. "I have nothing but time."

He hesitated, then looked at her closely. "Has Dr. Graves examined you?"

She nodded. "I was surprised when he told me the orphanage doctor had to leave. I was nervous at first, but Dr. Graves has a kind smile."

"Listen to Dr. Graves. He will make you feel better. And that will make Miss Chloe happy."

Emily sat up another inch and caught his gaze. "Do you like Miss Chloe?"

Very much. "We are friends."

They were, he realized. The physical attraction was still there, of course, and he couldn't imagine not desiring her. But she meant much more to him now. She was his confidant, someone who had seen him at his darkest moments and stayed by his side—his friend.

His future wife.

He wanted to tell Emily the happy news but kept silent. He knew Chloe would want to tell Emily herself, and he didn't want to ruin the surprise.

"I was friends with another girl," Emily said. "Her name was Caroline, but then she left with a handsome couple who wanted a girl, and she went away. I was happy for her, but sad at the same time. I'm old enough to know that a pretty lady and handsome man won't come and take me to their home. No one wants a sick girl."

Michael swallowed, and a sudden heaviness centered in his chest. Emily, if she was fortunate enough to overcome her illness, would most likely never be adopted but would live her life in the orphanage. She'd be one of the older girls he'd seen scrubbing the orphanage halls in exchange for their keep. If she did not fully recover, she could be sent to another institution or a hospital, a place with poor medical care where she wouldn't live long. He clenched his jaw. Dr. Graves would help the little girl. He had to.

Looking into Emily's intelligent green eyes, he saw what had drawn Chloe to the child. Yes, they shared a background. Both had been abandoned by a parent. Both had been ill—Emily still was. But there was more. They shared a similar spirt—a strength and resolve to survive, to fight. It's what he admired most about Chloe...and now Emily.

Michael pushed aside the nagging thought of Emily's illness and what it would do to Chloe if the child perished. He opened the book and began to read, "Once upon a time, there was a prince..."

Chapter Twenty-Two

The evening of Eliza's dinner party arrived quickly. "You look lovely," Henry told Chloe as he bowed over the hand she presented.

It took Chloe great effort to smile as Henry straightened and looked into her eyes. Guilt pressed heavily upon her chest. She wanted desperately to speak to him alone, but she'd have to be patient.

The room was full of guests waiting to enter the dining room. Her sisters and their husbands were sharing drinks and chatting amicably. Any private conversation would have to wait until after dinner when they could take a turn in the gardens.

A movement out of the corner of her eye drew her attention. She turned to see Michael enter the room and stand by the mantle. He looked every inch the powerful duke, and her breath caught in her throat. His meticulously cut jacket clung to his broad shoulders and emphasized the breadth of his chest. The rakish fall of dark hair across his brow made her want to run her fingers through it. Her eyes slowly rose to his, and a spark passed between them so strong she feared everyone in the room could see.

Their gaze was broken when Lady Willowby approached him. The widow looked stunning in a violet gown that clung to every curve of her voluptuous figure. The bodice was low, and an amethyst jewel the size of a walnut rested between her large breasts. She smiled up at him and touched his sleeve.

Chloe looked away as jealousy welled within her. She wanted to cross the room and rest her fingers on his sleeve, to stake her claim.

"Will you accompany me for a ride in the park tomorrow?" Henry asked, drawing her attention back to him. Henry was watching her with an expectant look on his face. She needed to tell him, and soon, but how best to go about it? "I'm afraid I have another dress appointment with my sister."

His looked crestfallen. "Another time?"

Her unease increased. "Henry, there is something I need to discuss with you. After the gentlemen enjoy their port and cigars following dinner, will you meet me in the gardens?"

Henry's eyes lit with anticipation, and he leaned forward to whisper in her ear. "I shall think of little else all evening."

Oh no. He believed she wanted a romantic tryst. She must end whatever false hopes he had between them.

She was saved from responding when the butler announced dinner was ready and the guests began to shuffle into the dining room.

Lady Willowby laughed flirtatiously as she took the duke's arm. Henry offered Chloe his arm as he escorted her into the dining room. Unable to avoid a glance toward Michael, her pulse pounded at his possessive stare.

It was going to be a long evening.

• • •

Chloe had no idea what she ate. As the wine flowed, she drank more than she should have. She was exhausted from making small talk with Henry, and she was forced to sit and watch as Lady Willowby cast Michael seductive glances and whispered in his ear. Like any good opportunist, she flirted outrageously with him throughout the entire meal. The attractive widow laughed, appearing to be avidly interested in whatever the topic of conversation was between them, her eyes widening in invitation. As the meal progressed and the footmen refilled their wineglasses, Lady Willowby grew bolder, leaning close to trace her fingers down the duke's sleeve to his bared wrist.

Chloe didn't know what was worse. Watching Lady Willowby fawn over the duke, or that Michael ignored her during the meal. She had no reason for her jealousy. She knew why he didn't glance at her, and that he wanted to protect her reputation until he could speak with Huntingdon and properly ask for her hand. If he paid her the slightest attention, then others may notice his interest, including Henry. Still, it took great effort and a good amount of wine to turn her attention away from the couple seated across from her and to pretend she was enjoying herself.

At long last, dinner ended and Chloe was one of the first to push back her chair. The men would remain in the dining room to enjoy their port and cigars, and the ladies would settle in the drawing room.

The brush of a hand on her low back caused a shiver of awareness to tingle along her spine. She turned to see Michael beside her and inhaled sharply. The look in his eyes was consuming and scorching at once, like a flame licking her skin. All thoughts that he'd been unaware of her vanished beneath his heated gaze. The corners of his lips curled in a tantalizing smile, and her heart pounded erratically in response. Her insecurities dissipated with that one heated look.

She hurried from the room and settled on a sofa in the

drawing room as Eliza began pouring tea. Chloe accepted her cup, and added a good amount of cream, two lumps of sugar, and then sipped the brew. She was still thinking of Michael's smile as Lady Willowby sat beside her and settled her silk skirts.

"Which one will it be, then?" the widow asked without preamble.

Chloe lowered her cup. "Pardon?"

The widow's painted lips curled in a mocking expression as she reached for her own teacup. She leaned close and lowered her voice. "Are you after the earl or the duke?"

"I don't know what—"

"The young earl is handsome and charming and willing to do whatever it takes to please. The duke is dominant and possessive and can heat a woman's blood with one dark glance. Who will it be?"

"None." Normally Chloe preferred directness. But in this case, she refused to give the woman the satisfaction of an answer.

"Don't insult my intelligence. We are both cunning women. I did not achieve my status by chance. I want the duke."

Over my dead body. Chloe's temper flared and rancor sharpened her voice. "Why are you telling me this?"

Cold green eyes sniped at her. "Because I see the way His Grace looks at you, and I don't like it."

"Perhaps you need to revisit *your* choice, then." She bit her lip to prevent herself from delivering another scathing response that she'd regret when her temper cooled.

She needed a moment alone to gather her thoughts and plan her next move. Amelia chose a seat beside Lady Willowby, so Chloe took the opportunity to excuse herself under pretense of seeking the ladies' retiring room.

She hurried down a long hall. The library's walnut-paneled walls, comfortable leather chairs, and its mahogany shelves full of books had always calmed her in the past. The room would offer a moment of tranquility before she must return to the group.

She rounded a corner, and the library door came into view. From the shadow of an alcove, a dark figure reached out to grasp her wrist. She whirled around.

Michael.

She pressed a hand to her pounding heart and gazed up at his dark visage. "Are you trying to scare me to death?"

He opened the library door, ushered her inside, then closed the door with a booted foot. "Finally. I have you alone."

She whirled to face him. "We cannot risk being caught alone like this," she whispered.

"You're right. I'm probably half mad." He stepped close and his gaze lowered to her mouth. Alarm slammed into her. Whether it was because of the tingle of excitement that warmed her blood at his nearness or her concern of being discovered she wasn't certain. "You should go before we are discovered missing."

"You mean by Henry or one of your sisters?"

"Perhaps Lady Willowby," she blurted out, then bit her lip.

He eyed her curiously. "Are you jealous?"

She raised her chin and glared at him.

An easy smile played at the corners of his mouth. "You have no reason to be jealous. I merely tolerated Lady Willowby so that the others would not suspect my affection for you. Now, are you going to tell Henry the truth, or shall I? I fear I cannot wait much longer. It's difficult to converse with Huntingdon and not tell him."

She squared her shoulders. "If you must know, I plan to tell Henry tonight outside in the gardens."

"Good. Because now that I have come to my senses and

proposed, it's hard to be in the same room as you and not touch you."

She couldn't suppress the lurch of excitement inside her, and her face grew hot from his words. "We must be careful. And you must be patient."

"You're right. I thought I'd mastered the virtue. Until you." He took another step forward, and her back pressed against the wall. He reached out but didn't cage her in, rather he caressed her cheek with the backs of his fingers—his touch infinitely gentle and seductive. His leg brushed the side of hers, and all her senses heightened. She saw the sharp cheekbones, the indent in his chin that made a woman want to press her lips there. She noticed the fine wool of his evening coat pull taut across his broad shoulders and caught the tantalizing scent of his cologne—sandalwood and cloves—and his unique masculine essence.

"What is it about you, Chloe Somerton?" His voice was a husky whisper, his gaze imprisoning hers.

Her lips curled in a smile. "What is it about *you,* Your Grace?"

He leaned in, and his lips hovered above hers. "I've never met anyone like you."

He pressed closer, and her breasts brushed against his broad chest. Her nipples hardened beneath the fabric of her gown, and her body ached for more of his exquisite touch. His breath heated her cheek, then his lips grazed the sensitive shell of her ear.

His voice was a husky whisper. "If I could toss you over my shoulder and claim you as my own, I would. Right here. Right now." She could see the torment inside him, the same warring emotions that coursed through her—desire, need, an emotional bond between two similar souls.

Despite her nervousness at being caught alone with him, his medieval, possessive words caused the blood to rush through her veins and heat her thighs and groin.

Goodness.

"I want to kiss you. May I?" he asked simply.

Her control was melting like snow in a hot bath. His hot touch…his seductive words…all served to turn her into a boneless mass of need.

"Say yes…"

In that instant, she forgot about the risk of discovery, forgot that her sisters were a few rooms away. The only person that mattered in the world was the man before her.

"Yes," she breathed. *Kiss me.*

At last he complied. Standing on tiptoe, she met his kiss. She welcomed him, parting her lips, and giving herself freely to the passion that raged through her. Her fingers clung to the soft wool of his coat before rising to sink into his thick, dark hair. His tongue met hers, gliding and exploring in a sensual swirl. His lips lowered to sear a path down her neck and throat, then the swell of her breasts above her bodice.

His hips pressed against her, his erection hard and demanding. She vividly remembered what it felt like to have him inside her, stretching her. Love flowed through her, and she wanted him again. Wanted more. Now that he'd shown her the pleasure to be had in his arms, she feared she would never be satisfied.

"Michael," she breathed.

He lifted her leg to wrap it round him, and she pressed against him in blatant invitation. His warm palm skimmed her calf, up her thigh, then stopped at the top of her garter where the bow ended and the soft skin of her thigh began. His touch made her wild in her skin, and she arched closer. His hand traveled higher, higher until his fingers parted her curls between her legs, and he touched her there. Pleasure rippled through her, and she released a cry that was part moan, part sigh.

"Ah, yes," he groaned.

He watched her, and desire darkened his eyes to almost black as he took in every gasp and his fingers worked their magic. The need to touch him grew. Reaching down, she cupped him through his trousers. He groaned low in his throat. Savage. Primitive. His fingers continued to stroke her, and she feared sliding down the wall in a pool of lust.

"Chloe," he rasped against the heated skin at her throat.

Deep in the recesses of her mind, she knew they were treading on dangerous ground. The risks were high. Discovery. Scandal. Ruin. But her inhibitions dissipated beneath the onslaught of his kiss...his touch...this aching need.

"Yes," she murmured against his skin. "Please don't stop."

His deep growl reverberated inside her.

The door slammed against the wall.

Michael pushed her behind him, shielding her with his frame. She was slower to come to her senses and realize someone else was in the room.

Dear God.

She peeked around Michael's broad shoulders to see Henry standing in the doorway. Henry, with his fair complexion—paler than she'd ever seen him.

Chapter Twenty-Three

Henry's wide eyes focused on them. "Christ!"

Chloe's heart thundered. "I'm so sorry…I wanted to tell you—"

"What? That you've been having an affair with the duke?" A sudden thin chill hung on the edge of his words.

"Henry," Michael said, his voice low but carrying a distinct warning.

"It isn't what it seems," Chloe blurted out.

Henry laughed, a high-pitched cackle that caused gooseflesh to rise on her arms. "What else could it be?"

How could she explain? She wasn't having an affair with the duke. Rather, she'd fallen in love with Michael. Madly in love.

She opened her mouth to speak, but Michael raised a hand. "We shall talk about this later, Henry. Right now, we need to leave before anyone else finds us."

Henry didn't seem to hear. His gaze was focused on her. "You behave the harlot for the duke."

Her stomach tilted. Her legs felt weak, and she would have

fallen if her back wasn't pressed against the wall for support.

"That's enough," Michael said tersely, his voice cold and clipped, and she saw a flash of the military commander in the harsh set of his jaw and the menacing look in his eyes. "Let's go, Henry."

"No, why should I? Perhaps I should call for Lady Huntingdon and enlighten her as to her sister's wanton behavior."

Michael's jaw tensed. "Listen to me, Henry. Chloe and I are to be married."

Astonishment crossed Henry's features. "Married?"

"I didn't want you to learn of it this way. I am truly story for not telling you sooner, but yes, we have decided to wed," Michael said.

Henry's shock yielded quickly to fury, and he glared at Chloe. "This is what you wanted all along, wasn't it? You'd be a duchess, far better than a countess as my wife."

"No!" she cried out. "I never meant to hurt you. I planned on telling you in the gardens tonight and explaining everything."

Henry's face turned a mottled shade of red. "I don't believe you or any of this." His lips thinned with anger. "Need I remind you, Your Grace, of the past?" He reached inside his waistcoat and withdrew a piece of parchment. From a distance, it appeared stained with dark ink.

"You gave this to me when you returned from Waterloo, and I carry it with me everywhere I go. You recognize it, don't you?"

A strange look crossed Michael's face. His mouth opened and closed, but he seemed to struggle to form a response.

"You must recognize the bloodstain. It was because of you," Henry said tersely, "that my father lies in a cold grave."

With pulse-pounding awareness, Chloe realized that the parchment was a letter—*the* letter Lord Sefton had carried on his person when he was killed saving Michael's life. The stain wasn't ink but dried blood.

A strange rasping sound echoed in the library. With rising dismay, Chloe realized it was coming from the duke, and she watched as his breathing grew labored.

"Stop it, Henry," she said. "Put that away. You must see what it's doing to him."

"I see, but I don't care. He *owes* me." Clenching the letter in his fist, Henry took a step forward and glared at the duke with burning, reproachful eyes. "Shall I read it out loud, Your Grace, or will you?"

A chill seemed to envelope the room. Michael's gaze lowered to the bloodstained parchment, and he stiffened. His eyes dilated. His jaw hardened like granite. His expression darkened with a fierce, faraway look. One that Chloe recognized all too well.

Chloe's heart pounded in dread. "Henry, stop," she demanded.

But Henry didn't notice the signs or heed her warning. He unfolded the letter and began to read in a clipped, tense voice, "To my closest friend, Lord Michael Keswick. If I shall perish in battle, then my last wish is for you to look after my son and sole heir—"

"Stop!" she repeated.

Henry's face was a glowering mask of rage. "You've never spoke of that day, Your Grace, and I demand the truth. Did my father cry out in pain when the bullet tore into his chest? Did he beg you to help him? Did you try to stop the bleeding yourself or call out for the army surgeon? Did you stay by my father's side as he took his last breath?"

Michael's chest heaved. His fists clenched at his sides, but he held still and seemed incapable of speech.

"Did you promise a dying man that you'd look after his only son, knowing you were lying? Did you?" At Michael's continued silence, Henry's temper flared. Clenching his teeth, he stepped forward and shoved the duke in the chest.

Michael still didn't respond. His attention was focused on the letter in Henry's hand.

"Answer me!" Henry shoved him again, this time with more force.

Again, no response.

"Coward!" Henry slammed the letter against Michael's chest. "You have no honor. Take this so that you never forget my father's sacrifice."

Michael flinched as if the parchment burned him through the layers of broadcloth and linen. He came to life then and tried to push the letter away, tried to evade Henry's grasp. But Henry was relentless.

A low menacing growl came from Michael's throat that caused gooseflesh to rise on her arms.

Oh no. She recognized that frightening sound. In his mind, he was on the battlefield. Just as when he saw Napoleon's carriage. Just as when the fireworks exploded in the gardens. But now, a physical reminder of that terrifying day had been thrust before him, was *touching* him.

It all happened swiftly. Michael's lips pulled back from his teeth and he wrapped his hands around Henry's throat. Henry's eyes bulged in shock.

Chloe lurched forward. "Michael! Stop!"

But Michael didn't look at her, his face twisted in anger. He was in the thick of battle, his blood running hot and fierce in a struggle for survival. He didn't know what he was doing or that it was Henry he was attacking. In his mind, it could be the French soldier who had shot and killed his best friend.

Chloe tried to pry Michael's hands loose, but she couldn't move him an inch. Henry wheezed.

Oh God.

The younger man didn't stand a chance against Michael's

superior strength. Henry began batting furiously at Michael's hands.

She needed to reach him, to bring him back to safety. "Michael, it's me! It's Chloe. You need to stop." She felt the slightest hesitation in him. "Let him go," she pleaded.

Just then, Henry flailed out in a desperate attempt to escape and struck her head. She cried out as a sharp pain pierced her temple. She stumbled back and reached out to grasp a chair, but missed. Her shoe snagged in the Oriental carpet, and she tripped and landed hard on the floor.

It was enough to make Michael halt. He reared back and dropped his hands from Henry's throat, then he looked down to where she lay sprawled and stunned on the library floor.

A flicker of emotion flashed in his eyes. Recognition? Confusion? He blinked and focused on her face. "Chloe?"

She reached for him, desperate to ensure he had returned. "Yes...yes... It's me."

He dropped to his knees beside her on the carpet.

At last, he let out a long breath and leaned back on his knees. His brows slashed downward, and he touched her temple. Pulling back, he stared at the blood on his finger. "Jesus. You're hurt."

She hadn't even realized she was bleeding. She touched herself and felt a cut on her hairline, and she suspected what had caused the injury. Henry's signet ring must have cut her when he'd flailed out. "I'm fine. It's not deep."

Henry stood behind them, his expression stark as he touched his throat. "I'm sorry, Chloe. I never meant for you to be harmed."

Michael didn't pay Henry attention. He helped her to her feet, his gaze traveling her from head to toe, then back to her face. He inhaled sharply. "You could have been gravely injured. Because of me."

"No, no. It wasn't your fault, and it's a small wound."

Her heart hammered in her chest. Instinct told her that she needed to quickly put his mind at ease.

He shook his head. "You could have hit your head and been taken from me," he said in a harsh, raw voice.

"No. It's nothing," she insisted. "Just an accident."

Henry remained still. "I should have heeded your warning to cease, Chloe. I never suspected it would go this far."

She felt Michael shudder as he drew in a sharp breath. "Go now, Henry. We'll talk about this later."

Henry hesitated for a heartbeat, long enough for Chloe to worry that he'd refuse to go once again. But then he nodded and crossed the room. He closed the door quietly on his way out.

Michael's complexion was ashen, and a look of tired sadness passed over his handsome features. "Christ. I should have known it was too good to last."

A warning voice whispered in her head. "What do you mean?"

He ran a shaky hand through his hair. "I was selfish to think I could have you forever. I cannot risk your safety. What happened here tonight proves I'm unfit for—"

She became more uneasy as her dismay grew. "As I said, you mustn't blame yourself. The letter was a physical reminder of that tragic day, and Henry should never have used it as he did. *You* didn't harm me, and I'm fine."

"No. Listen to me, Chloe. You need a man, one who is stable and competent. One who is in charge of his mind and body."

"I have one."

He shook his head. "I was a fool to think all would be well and that there was hope."

"There is *always* hope."

"Tonight proved that's false. What if this happens again? What if I go back to that dark place?"

"Then we will handle it together."

His jaw tensed. "No, we won't. I will handle it. Alone. I cannot marry you. I will not marry anyone."

Tears welled in her eyes. She swallowed hard, trying to manage a feeble answer. "Michael, please. You must not say such things."

"I'm truly sorry for what I have put you through, but I am not the man for you. Live your life, Chloe Somerton. Marry and have children. Forget me."

She grew desperate and reached for him, but he evaded her gasp. Her throat ached with anguish. "Michael—"

"Wait ten minutes, then return to the group."

"Wait! Don't leave me."

He glanced back. "I cannot…I will not change my mind." Then he turned and strode out the door.

Chloe stared at the closed door in shock and dismay. Then, slowly, she sagged and slid down the wall until she was curled in a ball on the Oriental carpet. Her fingers trembled as she touched her lips. They were still swollen from the duke's passionate kisses.

How had things turned so quickly? Happiness had been within reach. Her future had never been brighter. One minute she was in his arms, passion overriding reason, the next had been a nightmare. She'd finally found a man who cared naught for her past and wanted to marry her, only to lose him so quickly.

She loved him with all her heart, and he'd rejected her.

Her misery was a steel weight, and she felt the nauseating sickness of despair grip her. Life was truly cruel. How would she survive the evening? How would she survive at all? Her heart ached at the loss, and she wanted to flee—to shut herself in her bedchamber and succumb to wracking, soul-drenching sobs.

Only she could not. No one must suspect the truth. Instead, she wiped her eyes and returned to the party.

Chapter Twenty-Four

"What on earth is going on with you?" Eliza asked.

Chloe squirmed beneath Eliza's gaze. As soon as the last guest had departed, Chloe had fled to her bedchamber. But her relief was short-lived when both Eliza and Amelia had knocked on the door moments later. Chloe had anticipated their visit, and with Alice's assistance, she'd cleansed the small cut at her temple and concealed it by removing the pins in her hair.

Eliza pinched the bridge of her nose. "First Lord Sefton abruptly up and leaves, then the duke soon afterward."

"What makes you think I had something to do with it? Maybe the two of them had a disagreement?" Chloe wasn't ready to confess the truth to her sisters. She didn't think she could ever bring herself to talk about it.

Eliza rolled her eyes. "Don't be daft. You left the drawing room and didn't return for a long time. It doesn't take a genius to put two and two together."

Amelia made a face. "Don't forget that Lady Willowby complained all evening after the single men had departed."

Chloe could only imagine the widow's temperament. She'd been disagreeable after the duke had left Vauxhall Gardens unexpectedly and Lord Sefton was still present. With both eligible bachelors leaving early tonight, Chloe was surprised that Lady Willowby, also, hadn't stormed out of the house.

Eliza crossed her arms and impatiently tapped her foot. "Well?"

She feared telling them about the duke. Heaven only knew if Eliza would go straight to Huntingdon and tell her husband everything. Huntingdon would demand that the duke act honorably and force him to the altar. No, that wasn't what Chloe wanted at all. Michael would surely resent her.

But she owed her sisters an explanation about Henry.

"There's something I must tell you both, but I'm uncertain how to say it," Chloe admitted.

"Just tell us," Amelia prodded.

Chloe took a deep breath. "I'm no longer interested in marrying Lord Sefton. I think of him only as a friend, and I'm certain we'd make each other unhappy if we were forced to wed."

She was still reeling from the shock of his discovery. She'd never forget the look of betrayal on Henry's face. She never wanted to hurt him, and her stomach was still in knots. Would he reveal the scandal? All it would take was one word, one whisper, and he'd have his revenge. It was a risk, but she did not believe Henry would go so far. He may have been surprised to find her in the duke's arms, but he must have been even more stunned from Michael's episode.

"I knew it," Eliza said. "It's Lord Fairchild, isn't it? I saw you speaking to the red-haired man at Lady Webster's garden party."

Chloe was taken off guard by her sister's unexpected statement. "I...did speak with Lord Fairchild then, but—"

"It's not Lord Fairchild," Amelia said in exasperation. "The Duke of Cameron looks at you the way Lord Vale looked at me when we first met. Completely infatuated and determined not to take no for an answer."

Eliza's spine stiffened, and she looked at Chloe in shock. "Why haven't I noticed? I feel left out. Amelia has just returned, and she sees what must have been right under my nose. No wonder Lady Willowby had a sour expression all evening. Does *everyone* know?"

Chloe shook her head. "It doesn't matter. The duke has no wish to marry. I, on the other hand, have always wanted to find a suitable husband, remember?" Her words sounded hollow and shallow, and she couldn't fathom pursuing that goal any longer. She cared naught about snaring a rich, titled man now. If she couldn't have her duke, then how could she marry another?

So much had changed.

"She has a point," Eliza said. "I can only hope that's why I never noticed. I was focused on finding a husband for Chloe."

Amelia's eyes narrowed. "The duke told you that he doesn't wish to marry?"

"Yes," Chloe replied.

"That's ludicrous. He's a duke. He *has* to marry. It must be because of our father. We'll never be free of Jonathan Miller's sins," Amelia said bitterly.

"No. It's not Father," Chloe countered. "The duke suffers from aftereffects of the war."

Eliza frowned. "He was wounded? I didn't notice and I haven't heard—"

"Not physically," Chloe said. How best to explain Michael's torments? "It's more in his mind. He believes it unfair to subject a wife and child to his illness."

"Hmm. There are plenty of young ladies who'd trade their soul to become a duchess, even if he does suffer mental effects from the war. And the duke is no hardship on the eyes," Eliza said.

"I'm not convinced. Huntingdon wouldn't give you up, would he?" Amelia looked at Eliza. "And I know Vale wouldn't let me go. So if my instincts are right, I don't think the duke would be able to sit back and watch you marry another man, Chloe."

Chloe rubbed her forehead. "Well, your instincts are wrong in this case." *Terribly wrong.*

It was all a bloody mess, and Chloe's head began to pound. "I feel unwell. The stress of the evening has given me a headache."

Eliza and Amelia looked at her in concern, and their overprotectiveness took over. In their eyes she was still their little sister.

"I'll send for Alice," Eliza said.

"I'll tell her to fetch you a cup of warm milk," Amelia said as both sisters left the room.

At long last, Chloe was alone. She sat at her dressing table and rested her head in her hands. She gulped and then finally yielded to the compulsive sobs that shook her. Sleep and warm milk wouldn't help her tonight. Nothing would. There was no cure for a broken heart.

• • •

Michael sat in a chair before the hearth of his study, a decanter of scotch beside him. He raised the crystal decanter and filled his glass to the brim. He was well on his way to becoming drunk.

God, he hated what he'd done tonight. The wounded look in Chloe's blue eyes would haunt him all his days. He reached for the glass, took a swallow, and watched the fire in the grate.

He didn't have a choice. One glimpse of that dammed

letter had sent him back in time to the battlefield. Only Chloe's cry of pain had returned him to his senses. But by then, it was too late. She'd been hurt. It didn't matter that he hadn't delivered the blow. Her injury was a direct result of his actions.

It could have been worse. Much worse. His fingers curled around the glass. He should have dragged Henry from the library, out of Huntingdon's house, and explained everything. Michael owed it to him, owed it to Henry's father.

Henry had been right. He had no honor.

Michael threw his head back and downed the remaining contents in one swallow. The letter sat upon his desk. He dared a glimpse at it, and to his surprise his stomach didn't sink. Instead, he envisioned Chloe on the desk, her passionate cries as she experienced pleasure. Memories of her were everywhere in this room. They'd made love on the carpet before the hearth. They'd talked—first about his past and then about hers. His maps, his history books, his globe…even that damned letter on the desk didn't bother him now. Rather, he was filled with *her* presence.

He refilled his glass. No sense wanting what he could never have.

He cared for her too much to damn her to a life of hell. Only a selfish bastard could doom a woman like Chloe to a life of misery. If she was hurt tonight, then she risked far greater injury when he suffered another fit.

And he would.

It was as inevitable as the lowering of the sun each evening.

She should be happy, not constantly worried about him. For the first time, he'd done the right thing. The honorable thing.

Then why did it hurt so much?

Chapter Twenty-Five

Chloe woke feeling miserable. Her mind burned with the memory of Michael's kiss. Then, with a shiver of vivid recollection, the erotic images changed and she pictured Henry's stricken face as he'd walked into the library. She rose twice in the middle of the night to pace her bedchamber, then lie back down, only to have her mind return to its tortured thinking.

She pushed aside the coverlet and sat up in bed. There was only one place she wanted to be today. Only one person whose smile could always fill her with joy.

Chloe summoned her maid and dressed quickly. It wasn't her day to visit the orphanage, but she needed to visit Emily. A short carriage ride later, she arrived at the orphanage.

Her knock was answered quickly by a young girl, and Chloe hurried inside. The halls of the orphanage were empty, and she knew the children would be outside playing and she'd have time alone with Emily. Chloe entered the room that housed the younger girls and halted. A portly man was bent over Emily's bed, and he held a stethoscope to the child's chest. A medicine bag was open and rested on a nearby chair.

Chloe frowned. From what Mrs. Porter had told her, the orphanage physician would not visit Emily again until next week.

The man lowered the stethoscope and turned to Chloe. Blue eyes beneath bushy eyebrows and a slightly protruding brow met her gaze. Chloe was surprised to recognize Dr. Graves, the physician who had been at the duke's residence.

"Dr. Graves?" Chloe said as she approached the bed.

He lowered his stethoscope. "Ah, yes. You're the young lady I met at the Duke of Cameron's home. Miss Somerton, is it?"

Chloe nodded then glanced at the bed to see Emily's beaming face. "Miss Chloe! Have you come to read to me today?"

"Yes, sweetheart. Please pardon us, Emily, as I'd like a word with the doctor."

Dr. Graves closed his bag and followed her into the hall outside the room.

"Are you the new orphanage physician, sir?" Chloe asked.

"No, miss. I was sent to treat Miss Emily and offer a second opinion on her condition."

Chloe didn't think the orphanage could afford the services of another doctor, and neither Mrs. Porter nor Mr. Whitleson had mentioned they would hire another physician. Was Dr. Graves providing charitable services for free? Or was Michael somehow involved? She regarded the doctor with somber curiosity as the question intrigued her.

"Are you a friend or distant family of the child?" he asked her.

Chloe nodded. "A close friend. I have grown quite attached to young Emily. What can you tell me about her condition?"

"Today was my first visit with her and, although it is

too soon for a complete diagnosis, I believe the tonic the orphanage doctor has been treating her with is contributing to her decline. I recommend they cease the tonic and give her my medicine instead. She also needs to get outside. Being cooped up inside this old building is not conducive to anyone's good health, let alone a sickly child. I understand physical activity causes her shortness of breath, but I do believe fresh air will do her lungs wonders."

"Emily would love to go outside," Chloe said. How many times had Emily mentioned hearing the other children playing outside with longing in her voice?

"I will leave strict instructions for her care, and I shall return each day to check on the child. I understand there might be a conflict with the orphanage physician, but I'm confident if my treatment is followed, Emily will see the benefits."

Chloe wanted to kiss the man's shoes. "If funds are an issue, I will personally contribute what I can."

"There's no need. His Grace has more than generously paid for my services in advance."

Even though the thought had crossed her mind, she wanted confirmation. "His Grace? You mean the Duke of Cameron?"

"He seeks to keep his donations anonymous, but I suspected you already knew the truth after you saw me at his home."

Michael had visited the child once, only once, and he'd suddenly become Emily's benefactor. Why? Was it because of her?

"You said donations. Is there more?" she asked.

Dr. Graves smiled. "You are intelligent to catch my choice of wording. The duke has also made a sizeable donation to the orphanage to benefit all the children."

Chloe's emotions warred between shock, confusion, and gratitude. She loved Michael with all her heart. He was far from the coldhearted duke she'd initially believed. He was caring and generous. He did nothing to suffer the demons of his past.

Unlike her.

Too quickly, the old bitter feelings of unworthiness rose in her chest. She didn't deserve to be Michael's duchess. She knew why he'd changed his mind about marriage. He thought he was a danger to her because of his condition, not because of her past, but it didn't stop her old feelings of shamefulness from arising. She dropped her lashes quickly to hide the hurt from the doctor.

Dr. Graves turned to glance inside the room. "I'm afraid Emily is fast asleep. The medicine makes her drowsy."

"Thank you," Chloe said. "I shall sit with her until she wakes."

Dr. Graves handed her a paper. "If you ensure that the staff follows these instructions, I believe the child will improve. I shall return tomorrow." The doctor hurried down the hall, leaving Chloe alone with her thoughts.

• • •

Michael woke late with a pounding headache and wanted nothing more than to barricade himself in his study for the remainder of the day. But first, he knew he needed to check on Henry. He hadn't seen the young man since the debacle at Lady Huntingdon's gathering. He should ensure, at the very least, that Henry had not succumbed to the same urge and drunk himself into a stupor last night.

Michael opened his bedchamber door and surprised his staff when he summoned his valet. He bathed, shaved, and changed, and was on his second cup of coffee in the dining room when Hodges stepped inside.

"Lord Sefton is here to see you, Your Grace."

Michael was surprised. He wouldn't have to run around town inquiring about Henry's whereabouts after all. "Send him in."

Henry's eyes were bloodshot and his fair hair messed as if he'd run his fingers through it repeatedly. His normally neat attire was rumpled and his cravat loosely tied.

"Did you spend the entire evening drinking whisky at White's?" Michael asked.

Henry grimaced. "No, I spent the entire evening at home drinking whisky."

Michael motioned to a chair. "Sit. There's coffee."

He poured Henry a steaming cup, and Henry sipped it gratefully.

"Henry, I apologize for everything. I should have told you about Chloe. You know that I owe your father a debt I can never fully repay," Michael said.

Henry held up a hand. "I owe you an apology as well. I should never have used my father's letter as I did yesterday. As for a debt, there is none, Your Grace. My father thought highly of you and considered you a great commander and friend. He chose to save you that day at Waterloo. I suspect, were he given a choice, he would do the same again."

Michael's vow weighed upon him and his gut tightened. "I swore to look after—"

"Let me finish," Henry said, lowering his cup. "I've thought a lot about everything that occurred after last night. You have given me more than I can ever repay. You were there for me when my father didn't return from war. You taught me how to properly handle my new responsibilities that accompanied the title. I would have made a mess of the complicated estate ledgers and the numerous properties without your guidance."

"It's the least I could do. I have a head for figures and occasionally aided my father with the ledgers, and I had experience ordering supplies for my men in the army."

"Nonetheless, I would have disappointed all the servants and tenants who depend on me now. You have been more patient than my own father would have been."

"It was an honor. You need not thank me," Michael answered him thickly.

Henry looked at him for a long moment, pale blue eyes measuring him until Michael felt uncomfortable. "I've known that you've suffered from the war. My father may have failed to return, but you weren't unscathed. I've never brought it up, but still, I knew of it. There have been times I've stopped by and your butler informed me that you weren't receiving because you were…unwell."

He wasn't surprised Henry had suspected, and he was thankful he'd never inquired. A man didn't go around talking about his problems or his weaknesses. And in his case, his weaknesses were many. War heroes didn't have nightmares. British officers didn't wake up at night in a cold sweat, panting, hanging their heads over the side of the bed, casting up their stomach's contents.

"I've noticed the signs. You torment yourself. You can't sleep. You eat little and you drink too much. I've seen you leave a room when the topic of war arises, and I've seen you sweat and panic when you see something as harmless as Napoleon's carriage."

Michael's fingers tightened on his coffee cup, and Henry nodded. "That night at Vauxhall Gardens when you left abruptly, something else happened to you, didn't it?"

"Yes." Michael's voice was hoarse, uneven. He didn't want to go into the details. He hated talking about his fits, hated admitting to the weakness. "Chloe helped me that night. She saw me home so that no one would notice that I wasn't well."

Henry nodded. "I suspected as much. And last night proved all my suspicions true."

Michael felt ill at the reminder. "I want you to know that

I didn't consciously try to harm you."

"I know."

"I'm dealing with my condition."

"Other than last night, which I take responsibility for provoking you, I believe you. I have noticed a change in you as of late. You seem improved, relaxed, *happy*. If Chloe Somerton has helped you, then for that reason, I owe her my gratitude."

"Your gratitude?"

Henry held his gaze. "Yes."

Michael's thoughts turned to when Chloe had arrived in his study and helped him through a trying time. She'd offered him comfort and understanding. *Let go of your past. Guilt will only cripple you.* Miraculously, he had started to release the guilt. He'd found solace speaking about the worst day of his life, in the smooth strokes of her hands, in the sweetness of her giving body.

She'd helped him more than anyone in his life.

"When I learned of your relationship, my pride was wounded," Henry said.

Michael's gaze snapped to his. "We never intended to hurt you."

Henry lowered his cup. "My pride, but not my heart."

Relief coursed through Michael. He didn't want Henry to love Chloe. He didn't want any man to love her.

"I also came today to give you my blessing."

Michael stilled, his emotions vacillating between surprise and admiration. "That's no longer necessary. There will be no wedding."

"You changed your mind. Why?"

"It's not so easy."

"But it is. From what I surmised, she already agreed. Why change your mind?"

Michael ran a hand down his face. He'd gone berserk

when Henry had waved the bloody letter in his face. Every muscle in his body had tightened, and pressure in his chest had squeezed unbearably until animal instinct had taken over and he'd lunged for Henry. His actions had irrevocable consequences.

Good God. He believed that he'd had a breakthrough with her in his study. He'd actually thought there was a chance his condition could improve with time and patience, and he had hope for a future. A future with her. What a fool he'd been.

"It's complicated."

"Why?"

Michael's jaw tensed. "You saw for yourself. The war has left me…unbalanced."

"Last night was an accident, and I should never have shown you my father's letter. You cannot possibly think that you would purposely harm her."

He hoped to God he'd never intentionally harm anyone during one of his fits, but there was the emotional harm that he'd certainly cause. "She has already known loss when her father abandoned her. I would be no different."

"I don't believe you would, and deep down I think you know it as well. Are you willing to just walk away?"

The thought made his jaw clench. His need for Chloe went deeper than just physical attraction. She was a part of him, she didn't judge him or pity him, but rather, she understood. She'd foolishly thought her youthful sins made her unworthy when he found them admirable. Her past had forged her into an incredibly strong woman. A desirable woman.

The perfect woman for him.

"If there is one thing I've learned from this entire experience it is that love is rare and special," Henry said. "A man does not get to choose with whom, or when, he falls in love. Only the lucky ones get to grow old sharing the same pillow with a woman they love. And it may not happen to everyone. But when it does, you must seize it like the precious thing that it is. To walk away from it is a crime."

Henry's words struck him in the gut. He longed to hold Chloe through the night and wake each day beside her. His tormented soul wasn't entirely healed, he knew that, but she was the only one who had begun his path to his recovery.

He loved her. Totally and completely, he loved her. Looking back, he realized his feelings for her had begun the very first time she'd visited his home, stood up to him, and boldly told him she'd filched a man's purse rather than bother with his handkerchief. But that was why he was walking away. For her. For her future. She deserved better than a broken man.

"You have matured into a good man, Henry. Your father would be proud," Michael said.

"Thank you, Your Grace. My father would have wanted you to be at peace."

Michael felt his throat close up at the mention of his old friend. "And what about you?"

Henry chuckled. "I received an invitation this morning from the charming Lady Willowby to attend an intimate gathering at her home."

Michael suspected the shrewd widow had moved on to her next conquest. He wasn't alarmed. He was learning to trust Henry's judgment. Perhaps Lady Willowby would be a perfect match for him. "Good luck with the widow."

Henry stood and walked to the door, then turned to look back. "I can only hope you come to your senses. Don't let happiness slip through your fingers."

Michael pushed back his chair after Henry departed. Henry didn't understand. Happiness had to be shared. He couldn't be that selfish. He loved Chloe with all his being.

That's why he had to let her go.

Chapter Twenty-Six

Chloe arrived home from the orphanage to find Eliza and Amelia in the breakfast room. Their husbands weren't present, and the two sisters were enjoying cups of tea in the lovely, sun-drenched room.

"Come join us, Chloe," Eliza called out.

Chloe's nerves were frayed after everything that had occurred, but she knew her sisters would be concerned if she refused to join them. She chose a chair, and a footman set forth a cup of steaming tea before her then quietly left the room.

"How's Emily?" Amelia asked.

"For the first time, there is hope. The duke sent his own physician to treat her." Chloe did not have the opportunity to thank Michael for sending Dr. Graves to see Emily. Would she ever get the chance?

No. It was best if she didn't see him again. She'd never forget the determined look on Michael's face when he'd rejected her in Huntingdon's library.

Chloe cleared her throat and looked at her sisters. "There

is something else I must tell both of you. A secret I've kept to myself for far too long." She'd always believed she could keep her darkest sins from her sisters. But things were different now, and she'd withheld her past for too long. She was tired of the secrets, tired of carrying the burden.

Amelia lowered her cup. "Your secret has to do with the Duke of Cameron, doesn't it? We know you have strong feelings for him."

Chloe bit her lip. "It no longer matters."

"Of course it does, darling," Eliza said, reaching out to touch her hand.

Chloe felt like an ungrateful wretch. Her sisters were always her champions. "That's not what I want to discuss. The duke, I mean. My secret goes back years to when I was sick and a burden on both of you, financially and emotionally."

Both Amelia and Eliza looked confused and stricken. "You were never a burden," Amelia said.

"It's true. Never say such a thing," Eliza admonished.

"I felt like I was," Chloe said, casting her eyes downward. "I was always sick with that lingering cough and never able to work as hard as both of you in the print shop."

"You are the youngest. It was *my* responsibility to care for *you*," Eliza said firmly.

Chloe didn't want to argue, she just needed to tell them the truth. "I did something horrible. You will both look at me differently when I confess."

"It's clear something has been a burden on your shoulders. Tell us," Amelia urged.

Chloe took a deep breath. "I picked pockets. I stole from the wealthy shoppers on Bond Street."

"Why on earth would you do that?"

"I wanted to help pay for the cost of my cough tonic with Mr. Allenson at the apothecary. I know it was very costly and I...I *needed* to help any way I could." Chloe's voice sounded weak to her own ears.

"So you stole?" Eliza said. "I always wondered why the price of the tonic decreased over time. When I inquired, Mr. Allenson said the cost of the special herbs to make the medicine fluctuated. I thought he was being kind to our situation."

"He wasn't," Chloe said.

"But there's more, isn't there?" Eliza asked. "Mr. Allenson wouldn't accept anything but coins. Did you only steal purses from rich gentlemen?"

Always the shrewd businesswoman, Eliza caught on faster than Amelia when it came to the finances.

Chloe swallowed. The rest of the story was worse. "You're right. Mr. Allenson only wanted money. I traded the stolen goods for coins from Madame Satine at the Seven Sins brothel."

A horrible silence descended.

A heartbeat passed, then Amelia threw back her head and laughed. "And I thought I was the only one who felt sinful for following in father's footsteps and painting forgeries of priceless artwork."

Eliza looked more taken aback, but then she took a deep breath. "And I thought I was the most deceitful when I repeatedly lied, assuming the false identity of a widow to open the print shop."

Chloe looked at her sisters in astonishment. "You don't blame me?"

"How can we when we've all committed scandalous misdeeds? I do believe we should call ourselves the Infamous Somertons," Amelia said.

"The only thing we can blame you for is your foolish belief that you were ever a burden to us," Eliza said.

A huge sense of relief overwhelmed her at their understanding and compassion. Her sisters' love and acceptance wrapped around her like a warm blanket. The words came easier now. "You were right about the duke. I've fallen in love with him."

"That's wonderful, darling! Has he secretly proposed marriage?" Eliza asked.

"He did."

Eliza beamed. "Then he must speak with Vale and Huntingdon."

Chloe shook her head. "No. He has changed his mind. I told you about his war sickness. There was a confrontation with Henry the night of your dinner party. I jumped between them and there was an accident. I was pushed aside, but it was not the duke's fault. Henry flailed out and I suffered a minor injury." Chloe removed her bonnet and pushed her hair aside to reveal the wound.

Amelia placed a hand over her heart. "Are you all right?"

"Yes. It's a small wound," Chloe said.

Eliza's eyes narrowed. "Has Lord Sefton harmed you in any way before?"

Chloe's cheeks grew warm. "No, of course not. It was an accident."

"Thank goodness."

"You love the Duke of Cameron," Amelia said simply.

Chloe's face crumpled. There was no sense denying it. "It doesn't matter. He feels responsible for what occurred and deems himself unfit for a wife and children."

"Don't be so sure. He loves you," Amelia said.

Chloe merely shook her head. "He's never said a word."

"Darling, a dominant male like the Duke of Cameron won't come out and proclaim his love. He is a former military officer, a man trained to act on the battlefield. Let his actions speak for his heart."

Could it be true? Did Michael love her? He'd never spoken the words. She knew he admired her, desired her, and had wanted to marry her. He was also grateful for her aid. But did he truly love her?

Doubts crept in.

"You deserve happiness, darling," Amelia said.

Chloe twisted her fingers in her lap. "I need time alone to think. Perhaps I should return to the country. The fresh air will do me good." It was hard to believe that she'd only been in London for less than a month. So much had happened.

"Hmm," Eliza said. "It may not be a bad idea to return to Huntingdon's Hampshire estate for a brief respite."

A heaviness settled in Chloe's chest. "Yes, that would be best. Maybe I could travel. Didn't you receive a letter saying that Huntingdon's elderly aunt in Scotland is in need of a companion?"

"No need to flee the country," Amelia said.

"She's right," Eliza said. "Just a short visit to Hampshire is all we're agreeing to for now."

Chloe held her tongue. She doubted a short visit would be sufficient to heal her broken heart. She pushed back her chair. "I'll summon Alice and start packing."

Chapter Twenty-Seven

Of all the people Michael expected to visit his home, Lady Huntingdon was last on his list. She was waiting in the drawing room when Michael entered.

She turned away from the window overlooking the back gardens and curtsied. "Thank you for seeing me, Your Grace."

Michael bowed. "The pleasure is mine, Lady Huntingdon," he said as he motioned for them to sit in chairs before the gilded fireplace. "To what do I owe this pleasure?"

Lady Huntingdon smoothed her skirts. "I believe in being forthright. My sister, Chloe, has visited your home on several occasions."

He held her gaze, uncertain of her intent. "She has."

"Unchaperoned."

He recognized the keen intelligence in her green gaze and admired her for her straightforwardness. She had an air of calm, self-confidence, and he knew she'd been a shrewd businesswoman before marrying Lord Huntingdon. He also knew there was no sense lying to her. "Yes."

Lady Huntingdon nodded. "Chloe told us about her past.

All of it. She tells me that you also know."

"I do."

The beginnings of a smile tipped the corners of her mouth. "Chloe fancies herself in love with you."

His body vibrated with life. He'd never forget the moment she'd spoken the words to him in his library. She loved him. His breath had caught in his throat at the miraculous words. He wasn't worthy of such affection. "Lady Huntingdon, I—"

"Please, call me Eliza," she said.

"Very well, Eliza. I know about Chloe's past, and I assure you it means nothing to me. It's not her past that is the issue, but mine."

She tilted her head to the side and studied him. "Ah. I know about that, too. Your war experiences must have been tragic. My cook's husband, Ben, suffered after Waterloo."

She must have been referring to the soldier Chloe had mentioned.

"The last time I saw your sister at your home there was an altercation with Lord Sefton. You should know that Chloe sustained an injury, and that it could have been worse," he said.

"She told me about that, too. Other than a minor injury, she is fine. You do more harm to her by keeping your distance from her."

His determination faltered. "I'm thinking only of her. I live in fear that it could happen again."

"Chloe assures me it was an accident, and I trust her judgment. I also suspect you love her as well. I was slow to see it until my sister, Lady Vale, pointed it out to me. Artists can see much more than ordinary people."

He did love Chloe. Deeply, with all his heart. "That's why it is best if I stay away. I care for Chloe very much," he conceded.

"I must ask. Are you certain it is not her past that has

dissuaded you from considering her as your duchess?"

"No. Like I said, I care nothing for her past. But I was dismayed that she felt she had to keep it hidden for so long," he said.

Eliza's face fell. "I, too, am saddened that Chloe didn't tell us. I'm upset that she thought she was a burden to us. Looking back, I understand why she did what she did. She had it hard as a child. Always sick." Eliza sat back in her chair. "I want nothing but happiness for both of my sisters. That's why I'm here. You should know Chloe is set on leaving town."

His gaze snapped to hers. "Leaving?"

"She plans to return to Huntingdon's country estate. She even mentioned traveling to Scotland from there."

"Scotland?" he repeated dumbly.

"Huntingdon's aunt is elderly and needs a companion. I suspect she will overlook Chloe's talkative nature, should she even hear it, since I'm told she's mostly deaf."

Like hell. It wasn't fair that he'd experienced how it should be, how it could be, only to have it snatched away. No one else could offer him a chance at happiness. No one else could heal his battered soul and make him feel human again. And no one else could make him desire so fiercely.

Only Chloe.

And she belonged with *him.*

He'd been a fool.

A complete and utter fool.

Could he sit back and let her go?

The answer was a resounding no.

Eliza rose. "I fear I have said too much already and taken your time."

Michael leaped to his feet. "How soon is she planning to leave?"

She halted by the door and looked back at him. "She's packing as we speak. The coach leaves early tomorrow morning."

After Lady Huntingdon left, Michael remained in the room. He poured himself a glass of brandy, chose a leather chair, and started to plan. There was no way he could let Chloe leave London. Despite what she claimed, he knew deep in his gut that if she left the country to nurse an old woman in Scotland, it would *not* be temporary.

Chloe Somerton turned men's heads. Her cascade of golden hair, her sapphire eyes, and her curvaceous figure was a fascinating combination of allure and innocence that could tempt any red-blooded male. But it was her keen intelligence, her determination and strength that had enabled her to survive abandonment, poverty, and illness...and her empathy toward others that could capture hearts.

She'd be snatched up by a Scotsman before the end of her first week.

Hell.

He was ashamed that it had taken him so long to acknowledge his own feelings.

His illness still scared him—his dreaded, unpredictable episodes—but it didn't frighten him as much as losing her. The thought of living without her by his side was more terrifying than marching into enemy lines or standing in front of a loaded cannon.

He knew the perfect way to show her how much he cared. She may be willing to leave him behind, but there was a small child that Chloe could not ignore so easily.

He was counting on it.

• • •

Early the following morning, Chloe felt utterly miserable. The coach to take her to Hampshire would be arriving soon. It would be a long trip, stopping at numerous posting inns along the way, before she arrived at Huntingdon's country estate. She was grateful that her maid, Alice, was accompanying her. However, Chloe wouldn't be in the mood to talk, which meant she'd have mile after mile to think of Michael and what could have been.

She regretted that there wasn't enough time to say good-bye to Emily, but the orphanage didn't open its doors to visitors until early afternoon. Sweet, innocent Emily who bravely continued to fight her illness. She would miss the child terribly, and her only consolation was that Amelia and Eliza had agreed to visit Emily at the orphanage and explain that Chloe had to go on a trip. Her sisters had also agreed to visit the child weekly. Chloe had written explicit instructions as to the types of books and stories Emily preferred—fairy tales of princesses and, of course, dragons.

A fresh wave of longing sank in Chloe's stomach.

"Are you sure about this?" Alice asked. The maid was almost finished packing Chloe's stockings and shoes in a large trunk.

"Yes." *No.* She wasn't certain about anything. She only knew that staying in London without seeing Michael would be torture.

A low knock on her bedchamber door startled her. Alice opened the door to find a footman holding a letter. "This just arrived for you, Miss Chloe."

Chloe broke the seal and opened the letter.

Miss Somerton,

I am writing to notify you that Emily's progress has dramatically changed and the child is asking for you. Please come to the orphanage to see her before it is too late.

Respectfully,
Dr. Graves

Chloe felt the blood drain from her face as the letter fluttered to the carpet at her feet.

"What is it?" Alice asked.

"It's Emily. She's taken a turn for the worse and is asking for me. I have to go see her."

"But what about the coach?"

"There will be another. Quick! Help me dress and summon a carriage. There's no time to spare."

Chapter Twenty-Eight

Chloe sprinted up the front steps of the orphanage. She wiped a stray tear from her cheek as she ran down the hall that led to the room that housed the young girls and burst inside. She halted.

All the beds were empty.

Even Emily's.

Chloe ran to the back of the room to Emily's designated bed. The bed was neatly made with clean sheets, the brown blanket tidily tucked in all four corners.

She glanced around the room. The rest of the children would be outside playing, but Emily had been unable to join them in months. Good Lord, if the bed was empty, that could only mean one thing.

No!

Panic welled in her throat, and she rushed to the door and cried out. "Dr. Graves!"

Seconds later, Mrs. Porter rushed into the room. Her eyes were wide and her face flushed from running. "What's wrong, miss?"

"Where's Emily? Her bed is empty. Is she—"

"Outside, miss."

"*Outside?*"

"Yes, she's been feeling a bit better. A chair was taken outside, and the man carried Emily to join the other children."

"What man?" Chloe didn't wait for her response but threw open the door that led to the small garden behind the orphanage. She halted and blinked at the bright sunlight. Squinting, she shielded her eyes with her hand and scanned the lawn. The sounds of children laughing and playing reached her ears. A group of four kicked a ball back and forth. Several played with hoops and rolled them across the grass. Others played hide-and-seek—one boy was counting with his hand, covering his eyes while his playmates hid behind a hedge of bushes, a barrel, and trees. Emily was nowhere in sight.

A movement from the far end of the garden caught her eye.

Emily was seated in a chair, her glossy dark hair shining beneath the sun and her lips curled in a smile. A flash of white drew Chloe's attention, and she spotted a man squatting with his back to her. Then he stood to hand a daisy to Emily.

Chloe's heart hammered against her ribs as he turned and sunlight glinted on his dark hair.

She took a step forward just as Michael spotted her. He lifted a hand in greeting and grinned. A passionate fluttering arose at the back of her neck, and she found herself walking over to the pair.

"Miss Chloe, look what Mr. Michael brought for me today!" Emily held up a leather-bound book, the cover emblazoned with a fire-breathing dragon. "He said he searched three shops before he finally found one with a story that included a dragon and a princess. It's mine to keep."

"It's wonderful, darling. Are you certain you feel well enough to be outside today?"

Emily nodded. "The medicine Dr. Graves gave me has made me feel better."

A tear streamed down Chloe's face. This time, she didn't bother to wipe it away as she kneeled to hug Emily. "I'm so happy you feel well enough be outside."

"Dr. Graves said I will have to build up my strength, but that there is a good chance I may be able to walk on my own one day," Emily said.

A cry of relief broke from her lips. "That's wonderful!"

Emily was precious, and because Michael had cared enough to send his physician to treat the girl, she'd been given a second chance. Chloe knew that Emily wasn't miraculously cured, and that she would have a long, difficult journey ahead of her. But there was now hope, and it was all because of the man standing before her.

Gratitude and love welled in Chloe's chest. But it didn't explain why he was here today. Or the disturbing note from Dr. Graves.

Chloe stood and searched his handsome face. "I never had the chance to thank you for sending Dr. Graves to treat Emily. Why did you do it?"

Their gazes locked and he smiled. "Why have the power and riches of a dukedom if one cannot put it to good use?"

Chloe's heart hammered in her ears. She opened her mouth to answer when Emily tugged on her skirt and drew her attention. "I saved the best news for last. Mr. Michael said I could come live with him."

Chloe blinked. "Pardon?" She couldn't have been more surprised if Emily had risen from the chair and danced a jig.

Emily's eyes were bright with excitement. "He's taking me home. He says I'll even have my own bedchamber. Can you imagine?"

Why would Michael promise such a thing to the child? Had Emily misunderstood?

Emily continued chattering, oblivious to Chloe's shock. "He said you can live with us there, too."

Chloe's eyes snapped to Michael's face. He stood tall, watching her with his unfathomable dark eyes, revealing nothing and everything at the same time. She wavered on her feet. His hand grasped her arm to steady her.

"Emily, love," Michael said, "will you excuse us and watch the others so that I may speak with Miss Chloe in private?"

Emily giggled with an unmistakable twinkle of mischief in her eye. "Good luck, Duke."

Michael offered Chloe his arm. "Come," he said simply.

She had no choice but to follow him as he led her to the far side of the lawn until they were concealed behind a tall hedgerow.

As she looked up at him, her heart lurched madly. Must he be so handsome? "Are you serious about bringing Emily home with you?"

"I am."

"Why?"

"She needs a home. I have more rooms than I'll ever need." She still didn't comprehend. Dukes didn't just take home orphaned children. Did he intend for Emily to become one of his staff?

"Emily misunderstood. She thinks I'm coming along as well."

"There's no misunderstanding. I may own a mansion, but I have no clue how to raise a child."

"You are a duke. You can hire the best nannies and governesses in London."

"True. But Emily needs you. So do I."

She frowned, her head puzzled by what he was saying. She met his gaze and the deep longing in the depths of his eyes nearly took her breath away. She gasped, hope blossoming in her chest. "You can't mean—"

"I'm sorry for what I put you through. When I learned that you were leaving London, I realized what a fool I've been. Will you accept my apology?"

"How did you learn I was leaving?"

"Your sister Eliza paid me a visit."

Chloe's thoughts whirled. "Eliza…what about the note from Dr. Graves? Did you have something to do about that?"

"I needed a way to get you here."

Then the impossible, beautiful man knelt on one knee before her. "I must do this properly this time. Chloe Somerton, will you do me the honor of becoming my wife?"

Longing flared as bright as the afternoon sun inside her. She loved this battle-hardened man. All his flaws and his perfections. She wanted to throw herself in his arms, kiss him, and proclaim her love.

She had wanted to marry a rich, titled man for as long as she could remember, but the fact that Michael was a duke and wealthy as sin didn't account for her joy. She'd gladly spend the rest of her life with him if he were a struggling merchant, just as she had been years ago. He completed her as no other man. Little by little, warmth crept back into her body. His appeal was irresistible. She smiled at his arrogance and sheer confidence.

"I know that I'm not cured and will have moments where I will struggle. But I no longer fear my future, but look forward to it. With you by my side, I can face anything. Now, will you accept my proposal?"

Still, she needed to be certain. "Why? Tell me why you want to marry me."

A flicker of unease crossed his face, but it was quickly replaced with resolve. "Because you ease my soul. Because I can sleep peacefully for the first time in well over a year. Because I've been a fool not to see what was so obvious to me before. Because the thought of losing you terrifies me more than marching into battle. And because I love you."

Her heart leaped with joy. "Oh, Michael."

"Is that a yes? Please take pity on me and accept because my knee is starting to ache."

"Yes!" She threw herself at him just as he rose. Strong hands came around to grasp her waist, and his lips brushed her forehead. "You've made me the happiest man alive."

Her heart lurched madly. "I love you. I've loved you for so long."

"Say it again," he demanded fiercely.

"I love you."

"Thank God."

Hands clasped together, they stepped from behind the tall hedgerow to smile and wave at Emily across the lawn.

Emily laughed happily and waved back.

Chloe blew her a kiss. "What will you tell people about her?"

"That Emily is the daughter of a deceased cousin. I know we cannot claim her as our own, but I promise to treat her as one of ours."

She gave him a cocky smile. "One of ours? Does that mean you have decided you *want* children?"

"A dozen. You have cured me of that fear, my lady."

"Goodness! That's a rather large family."

"Then the wedding will have to take place quickly so that we can get started. I'm a duke, after all, and can obtain a special license. Henry shall be my best man."

"Truly?"

"We have his blessing. And deep inside, I know I have his father's as well."

He was perfect. She leaned up on tiptoe and kissed him. "Then I look forward to a new beginning."

Epilogue

Six Months Later

"Miss Chloe! Come see what the duke has brought home."

Chloe smiled at Emily and extended her hand. Together they walked to where Michael stood in the gardens of their Berkeley Square home. Chloe's eyes filled with tears when she thought of how far Emily had come. With Dr. Graves's care, her health had improved. She'd started to walk, a miracle for sure.

Michael had let it be known that Emily was a relation and no one had questioned it. As far as Chloe was concerned, Emily was their daughter.

Michael waved as the two women approached. In his arms was a black cloth bag.

They sat on a bench, and he joined them and set the bag on his lap. He looked as handsome as ever with his broad shoulders and dark eyes and hair, and she marveled that she was now his duchess. Their wedding had been the event of the Season. Eliza, Amelia, and Huntingdon and Vale had all been present.

The bag wiggled.

Emily's eyes grew large. "What is it?"

"Go on," he said. "Open it."

Emily reached out and pushed the black cloth aside to reveal a tiny kitten with jewel-green eyes. The feline was entirely black, except for four white paws.

"Oh! He's lovely. Is he for me?" Emily asked.

"It's a she, and yes." Michael removed the kitten from the bag and set the tiny creature on Emily's lap.

"Thank you!" Emily stroke the kitten's soft fur and was rewarded with a *meow*.

"What will you name her, darling?" Chloe asked.

"Stockings, for her white feet."

"Stockings. I like it," Michael said.

"May I play with her?" Emily asked.

"Of course," Michael said. "Cook has some fish and water inside."

Emily cradled the kitten in her arms and hurried into the house.

Chloe turned to Michael beside her. "That was very thoughtful of you."

A devilish look came into his eyes. "You may not thank me for long. Emily also wants a puppy."

"A wife, a child, a kitten, and a puppy," Chloe said, counting on her fingers. "That's four. You'd best be careful, Your Grace. Huntingdon and Vale will think you're smitten."

"Ah, I suppose I am. It's all your fault, love."

Her heart lurched madly. His vitality still captivated her, and she'd never grow tired of him or stop desiring him.

Thank goodness, Michael was doing better as well. His nightmares had almost ceased, and when he did suffer from a bad dream, he'd learned to wake her and together they would talk through his fears.

But there was one more thing he would need to overcome.

She cleared her throat. "Michael? There's something I must tell you."

He arched a dark eyebrow and stroked his fingers down her arm. "Is it another secret from your past? I assure you it won't matter one whit."

She slapped his hand away playfully. "It has nothing to do with my past, but *our* future."

He stilled, and his gaze rose to hers. "Chloe?"

"By the look on your face, I assume you've already guessed. I'm with child."

She held her breath. He'd broken his steadfast rule about marriage. He'd taken Emily into their home. But a baby? Would he be happy? Or would his old fears return?

Then he broke into a wide grin, and her nerves eased. "Truly?"

She nodded. "Yes. I'm certain, and Dr. Graves confirmed it."

He gathered her into his arms and kissed her, his lips warm and sweet on hers.

She pulled back slightly. "You're not afraid? Disappointed?"

"Disappointed? Never. Afraid? Yes. But also, joyous and thrilled. Thank you. I love you, Chloe, with all my heart.

Her heart welled with happiness. "I love you, too."

His expression grew serious as he held her. "For the first time, I don't regret my past. Without it, I would never have met you, the woman who has given me hope."

Acknowledgments

Writers create stories in solitude, but publishing a book is a team effort. I'm thankful for all the wonderful people who have helped me along the way.

Stephany Evans, my wonderfully supportive agent who knows how to make my books strong and who has helped my career. I'm eternally grateful!

Alycia Tornetta, my editor, who always helps to polish my books and make them shine.

Maryliz Clark, my longtime friend, beta reader, and fabulous grammar queen.

To all the people at Entangled Publishing who help with my beautiful covers and all the behind-the-scenes work.

To the Violet Femmes and the NJ Romance Writers for their friendship.

And to my family, for all their support, patience, and their love. Especially John. Love you all!

About the Author

Bestselling author Tina Gabrielle is an attorney and former mechanical engineer whose love of reading for pleasure helped her get through years of academia. She often picked up a romance and let her fantasies of knights in shining armor and lords and ladies carry her away. *Publisher's Weekly* calls her Regency Barrister series, "Well-matched lovers... witty comradely repartee." Tina's books have been Barnes & Noble top picks, and her first book, *Lady Of Scandal*, was nominated as best first historical by *Romantic Times Book Reviews*. Tina loves to hear from readers. Visit her website to learn about upcoming releases, join her newsletter, and enter free monthly contests at www.tinagabrielle.com

You can also find Tina at:

Twitter: @tinagabrielle

Facebook: www.facebook.com/TinaGabrielle

Instagram: instagram.com/tinagabrielleauthor/

Get Scandalous with these historical reads...

DENYING THE DUKE
a *Lords and Ladies in Love* novel by Callie Hutton

Alex returns to assume the title Duke of Bedford when his brother unexpectedly dies. He is unprepared for both his new responsibilities and the reunion with Patience, the woman he'd loved who had been betrothed to his brother. He has been to war and is a changed man. Doesn't Patience know that! Where is the man she loved gone? They must accept the changes or deny them and move on.

TO SEDUCE A LADY'S HEART
a *Landon Sisters* novel by Ingrid Hahn

Lord Jeremy Landon, Earl of Bennington is manipulated into marrying a spinster. Lady Eliza Burke is tired of living under the rule of a tyrannical mother, so much so that she will even marry a man she doesn't know, one her mother despises. Eliza doesn't believe herself destined for love. Jeremy doesn't believe he's destined for happiness. Their unexpected love must weather scandal and their own ingrained beliefs if it is to survive.

The Seduction of Sarah Marks
by Kathleen Bittner Roth

ENGLAND 1857

After a blow to her head, Sarah Marks awakens in a strange bed with a strange man and no memory of how she got there. Her handsome bedmate, Lord Eastleigh, tells her she's suffering from amnesia and the best course of action is to travel home with him until she recovers her memory.

Lord Eastleigh has his own reasons for helping Sarah and keeping her close. Reasons he cannot tell Sarah. As they struggle to restore her memory, their undeniable, inadvisable attraction grows—until Sarah finally remembers the one thing that could keep them apart forever.

Wicked in His Arms
a *Wedded by Scandal* novel by Stacy Reid

The last woman Tobias Walcott, the Earl of Blade, would ever marry is Lady Olivia Sherwood. She's everything he should not desire in a female—unconventional, too decisive, and utterly without decorum. But when he ends up trapped in a closet at a house party with her, passion ignites. Honor demands they wed, and while Tobias finds himself unwillingly drawn to the bewitching beauty, he must do everything not to tempt the passion that burns in him for her, lest it leads to disastrous consequences.

Made in United States
North Haven, CT
13 March 2024